TRIPLE PLAY

A Nathan Heller Casebook

The Memoirs of Nathan Heller

True Detective
True Crime
The Million-Dollar Wound
Neon Mirage
Stolen Away
Carnal Hours
Blood and Thunder
Damned in Paradise
Flying Blind
Majic Man
Angel in Black
Chicago Confidential
Bye Bye Baby
Chicago Lightning (short stories)
Triple Play (novellas)

TRIPLE PLAY

A Nathan Heller Casebook

MAX ALLAN COLLINS

PUBLISHED BY

🦅THOMAS & MERCER

Published by Thomas & Mercer
P.O. Box 400818
Las Vegas, NV 89140

ISBN-13: 9781612180922
ISBN-10: 1612180922

*A fedora tip to George Hagenauer—
whose work on these three Heller cases
deserves special thanks*

Although the historical incidents in these novellas are portrayed more or less accurately (as much as the passage of time and contradictory source material will allow), fact, speculation, and fiction are freely mixed here; historical personages exist side by side with composite characters and wholly fictional ones—all of whom act and speak at the author's whim.

TABLE OF CONTENTS

TRIPLE PLAY
An Introduction
by Max Allan Collins

Is there a difference between a novella and a novelette? Damned if I know.

But I do know that both seem to happen around the point where the very long short story meets the very short novel. It's a form that was once quite popular, often showcased by such major magazines as *The Saturday Evening Post, Redbook, Cosmopolitan, Liberty,* and *Collier's*. Even in the 1960s and early '70s, the classier men's adventure magazines—and being one of the classier men's adventure magazines, of course, didn't really make you very classy—would reserve the last section of their periodicals for novelettes, usually by famous mystery writers.

For many years, the great Rex Stout would write one Nero Wolfe novel and one Wolfe novelette a year, the latter for various "slick" magazine markets. When he'd done three of the short novels, he would collect them into a book; these novella collections bore such titles as *Triple Jeopardy, Three Men Out, Trouble in Triplicate,* and *Curtains for Three*. Stout is obviously very at home in the 20,000-word form, and the A&E *Nero Wolfe* TV series of a few years back often used the novellas as the basis for scripts. Stout lived to a ripe old age, leaving us a wealth of wonderful stories, but he also lived long enough to see the market for novellas dry up, and he, Nero Wolfe, and Archie Goodwin spent the last ten years of their collective career only in novels.

Mickey Spillane—during his self-imposed hiatus from writing Mike Hammer yarns (1952–1962) at the peak of his popularity—kept his hand in by writing 20,000-word tales for men's magazine the likes of *Cavalier* and *Saga*. The pulps were largely gone in the '50s and '60s, *Black Mask*—where Dashiell Hammett and Raymond Chandler cut their teeth—was already just a memory; but *Black Mask*'s successor, *Manhunt*, launched itself in 1953 with a four-part serialized Spillane mininovel. During its decade-and-a-half run, *Manhunt* often showcased short novels by Richard S. Prather, Brett Halliday, Cornell Woolrich, Ed McBain, Ross MacDonald, Charles Williams, and many other major writers of noir fiction of the 1950s and '60s.

Manhunt wasn't alone, getting competition from *Mike Shayne Mystery Magazine* and the still-going (if more genteel) *Ellery Queen's Mystery Magazine*, as well as a succession of short-lived digest-sized pulps wearing the names of writers (*Rex Stout*), famous fictional detectives (*The Saint*), and even TV series (*77 Sunset Strip*).

Many of the novellas published by *Manhunt* and its rivals wound up expanded into novels, sometimes appearing in hardcover but more often as paperbacks. Mystery novels of the mid-twentieth century were often short by today's standards—40,000 to 50,000 words. A number of paperback publishers followed the lead of Fawcett Publications' Gold Medal Books in putting out tough, sexy, hardboiled novels about PIs, crooks, cops, and (following the lead of James M. Cain's *Postman Always Rings Twice*) hapless ordinary guys caught up in crime and lust.

The mystery digests, and paperback houses like Gold Medal Books, were filling the void left by the pulps of the *Black Mask* era. Gold Medal was specifically formed to take advantage of the mostly male, post–World War II market unveiled by New American Library's enormously successful paperback reprints of *I, the Jury* and Mickey Spillane's other early Mike Hammer novels.

Much like Elvis Presley with rock 'n' roll, Spillane broke down barriers on sex and violence in popular culture that caused reverberations still felt today, and the sexy covers of the Hammer reprints set the standard and tone for Gold Medal and other publishers. In his hardcover mysteries, Spillane also wrote fairly short yarns—more like 60,000 words on average—but still the kind of swift, startling read that really caught and held a reader's attention.

As the years have passed, however, the short novel—even the 40,000–50,000 word variety—has become an endangered species. Occasionally a magazine like *Ellery Queen* will publish a longer story, as do anthologies of original material. Still, when I came along with my Nate Heller character in the early '80s, the demand for novelettes was right in there with the call for buggy whips and codpieces.

At first, writing short stories themselves seemed like a waste of time to me. You had to create stories "on spec," that is, just write the damn things, send them in to one of the handful of markets, and pray for acceptance. My agent wouldn't even bother with marketing short stories (still doesn't). With a novel, on the other hand, I could write a proposal and perhaps a sample chapter or two, and land a contract—sometimes a two- or even three-book contract. It still works that way more than a decade into the twenty-first century.

But in the '80s and '90s, original material anthologies became fashionable (and are still around, though starting to look like potential buggy whips and/or codpieces), and now and then I would be invited into a collection of original stories. When you're asked to the party, you have to really misbehave to get tossed out. I've never been invited to contribute a story to such a collection only to be rejected. As an editor of around ten anthologies of that ilk, I believe I only rejected one story, and perhaps asked for rewrites on half a dozen (of 150 or more stories). So as bets go in the writing game, an invite from an anthologist is a safe one.

Still, requests for novellas are rare. So far in my career—and Nate Heller's—I've only been asked to write short novels on three occasions. Two collections of my Heller short stories, by separate publishers, needed a new story to attract readers who'd already seen those previously published tales. In both cases, the editors requested a novella to both plump out the volume and to further make a purchase attractive to readers who already had some, or maybe all, of the rest of the stories. (Both of those "casebook" collections are out of print, and this volume—and *Chicago Lightning*, another short story collection from AmazonEncore—take their place.)

The idea of a short Heller novel appealed to me on any number of levels. The novels always take on major crimes and are massive undertakings of research and narrative. The short stories allow me to do chamber pieces, tackling small, un-famous crimes that would find Heller behaving more like a day-to-day detective, getting away from the admittedly ridiculous notion that every single case of his involves a world-famous crime.

A short novel, on the other hand, splits the difference. It allows Heller and me to take on a case that involves a famous crime or famous people but that doesn't quite qualify for the full-scale, 100,000-word treatment.

In "Dying in the Post-War World," I was able to take on the William Heirens "lipstick killer" case, which was well known but not really complex enough to justify novel-length treatment. This first Heller novella was approached as if I were writing a

Gold Medal paperback back in 1963, relishing the opportunity to take my detective into a format I'd grown up reading and loving.

One of the most interesting things about writing that particular novella was hearing by mail from the still-incarcerated William Heirens. For several years I received Christmas cards from him, from prison. What did the convicted lipstick killer think of the story? Well, he commended me for being fair, but said he "disagreed" with certain aspects of my take on the crimes. Which aspects, I think, should be clear to you once you've read the novella.

The circumstances of "Kisses of Death" are unusual. A small Chicago audio firm had been doing abridged versions of the Heller novels, with me reading. They wanted to promote these audiobooks at the upcoming 1996 American Booksellers Association convention in Chicago. They wondered if I could write a Heller novella set at the ABA, and then we'd record it, and give it away at their booth.

While the ABA does figure into the story, "Kisses of Death" is mostly about Marilyn Monroe, who I knew had worked on her autobiography (not published till many years after her death) with legendary Chicago writer Ben Hecht of *Front Page* fame. I'd long wanted to get Hecht on stage in the Heller saga, and had always known Marilyn would enter, when I moved out of the '30s and '40s into the 1950s. But I needed a literary murder to tie it all together—the audiobook was designed to be given away at the ABA event, after all.

My longtime research associate, George Hagenauer, came through, with an incident involving prototypical beatnik poet/ novelist, Maxwell Bodenheim. The Bodenheim case was exactly the kind of story suitable for a novella—too big for a short story, too small for a full-scale novel. Bodenheim also fit right in with Marilyn's own ambitions and pretensions toward becoming an intellectual.

I wrote the story, recorded it (with my lovely wife Barbara reading the Marilyn Monroe lines), and we gave away a bunch of cassettes at that year's ABA exhibition at Chicago's McCormack Place. It did not appear in print until 2001 when it became the title story of the second Heller casebook.

In "Strike Zone," I took advantage of a particularly peculiar crime—the murder of the most famous pinch hitter in history, who happened to be a midget—and also explored colorful base-ball legend Bill Veeck. George Hagenauer had known Veeck quite well, which was a big plus. This novella, the shortest of the three collected here, was written at the request of Otto Penzler for a baseball crime/mystery anthology. Another author had dropped out, and Otto needed a long story to help reach the anthology's overall required word count.

I was glad to help out, though I admitted to Otto—and will admit to you—that I am not a baseball fan. Few baseball references appear in the Heller memoirs (boxing is his sport of choice). My late father, Max A. Collins Sr., however, was one of the greatest fans of baseball (and sports in general) who ever lived, and I dedicate that story—and this book—to his memory.

—Max Allan Collins
February 2010

DYING IN THE
POST—WAR WORLD

1

Life was pretty much perfect.

I had a brand-new brown-brick GI Bill bungalow in quietly suburban Lincolnwood; Peggy, my wife since December of last year, was ripely pregnant; I'd bribed a North Side car dealer into getting one of the first new Plymouths; and I'd just moved the A-1 Detective Agency into the prestigious old Rookery Building in the Loop.

True, business was a little slow—a good share of A-1's trade, over the years, has been divorce work, and nobody was getting divorced right now. It was July of 1947, and former soldiers and their blushing brides were still fucking, not fighting, but that would come. I was patient. In the meantime, there were plenty of credit checks to run. People were spending dough, chasing after their post-war dreams.

Sunlight was filtering in through the sheer curtains of our little bedroom, teasing my beautiful wife into wakefulness. I was already up—it was a quarter to eight, and I tried to be in to work by nine (when you're the boss, punctuality is optional). I was standing near the bed, snugging my tie, when Peg looked up at me through slits.

"I put the coffee on," I said. "I can scramble you some eggs, if you like. Fancier than that, you're on your own."

"What time is it?" She sat up; the covers slid down the slope of her tummy. Her swollen breasts poked at the gathered top of her nightgown.

I told her the time, even though a clock was on the night-stand nearby.

She swallowed thickly. Blinked. Peg's skin was pale, translucent; a faint trail of freckles decorated a pert nose. Her eyebrows were thick, her eyes big and violet. Without makeup, her dark brown curly locks a mess, seven months pregnant, first thing in the morning, she was gorgeous.

She, of course, didn't think so. She had told me repeatedly, for the last two months—when her pregnancy had begun to make itself blatantly obvious—that she looked hideous and bloated. Less than ten years ago, she'd been an artist's model; just a year ago, she'd been a smartly dressed young businesswoman. Now, she was a pregnant housewife, and not a happy one.

That was why I'd been making breakfast for the last several weeks.

Out in the hall, the phone rang.

"I'll get it," I said.

She nodded; she was sitting on the bed, easing her swollen feet into pink slippers, a task she was approaching with the care and precision of a bomb-squad guy removing a detonator.

I got it on the third ring. "This is Heller," I said.

"Nate ... this is Bob."

I didn't recognize the voice, but I recognized the tone: desperation, with some despair mixed in.

"Bob ...?"

"Bob Keenan," the tremulous voice said.

"Oh! Bob." And I immediately wondered why Bob Keenan, who just a passing acquaintance, would be calling me at home, first thing in the morning. Keenan was a friend and client of an attorney I did work for, and I'd had lunch with both of them, at Binyon's, around the corner from my old office on Van

Buren, perhaps four times over the past six months. That was the extent of it.

"I hate to bother you at home ... but something ... something *awful*'s happened. You're the only person I could think of who can help me. Can you come, straightaway?"

"Bob, do you want to talk about this?"

"Not on the phone! Come right away. Please?"

That last word was a tortured cry for help.

I couldn't turn him down. Whatever was up, this guy was hurting. Besides which, Keenan was well off—he was one of the top administrators at the Office of Price Administration. So there might be some dough in it.

"Sure," I said. "I'll be right there."

He gave me the address (of his home), and I wrote it down and hung up; went out in the kitchen, where Peg sat in her white terry cloth bathrobe, staring over her black coffee.

"Can you fix yourself something, honey?" I asked. "I'm going to have to skip breakfast."

Peg looked at me hollow-eyed.

"I want a divorce," she said.

I swallowed. "Well, maybe I do have time to fix you a little breakfast."

She looked at me hard. "I'm not kidding, Nate. I want a divorce."

I nodded. Sighed, and said, "We'll talk about it later."

She looked away. Sipped her coffee. "Let's do that," she said.

I slipped on my suit coat and went out into the bright, sunny day. Birds were chirping. From down the street came the gentle whir of a lawn mower. It would be hot later, but right now it was pleasant, even a little cool.

The dark blue Plymouth was at the curb and I went to it. Well, maybe this wasn't all bad: maybe this meant A-1's business would be picking up, now that divorce had finally come home from the war.

2

The house—mansion, really—had been once belonged to a guy named Murphy who invented the bed of the same name, one of which I had slept in many a night, back when my office and my apartment were one and the same. But the rectangular cream-color brick building, wearing its jaunty green hat of a roof, had long ago been turned into a two-family dwelling.

Nonetheless, it was an impressive residence, with a sloping lawn and a twin-pillared entrance, just a block from the lake on the far North Side. And the Keenan family had a whole floor to themselves, the first, with seven spacious rooms. Bob Keenan was doing all right, with his OPA position.

Only right now he wasn't doing so good.

He met me at the front door; in shirtsleeves, no tie, his fleshy face long and pale, eyes wide with worry. He was around forty, but something, this morning, had added an immediate extra ten years.

"Thank you, Nate," he said, grasping my hand eagerly, "thank you for coming."

"Sure, Bob," I said.

He ushered me through the nicely but not lavishly furnished apartment like a guy with the flu showing a plumber where the busted toilet was.

"Look in here," he said, and he held his palm out. I entered what was clearly a child's room, a little girl's room. Pink floral wallpaper, a graceful tiny wooden bed, slippers on the rug nearby, sheer feminine curtains, a toy chest on which various dolls sat like sweetly obedient children.

I shrugged. "What ...?"

"This is JoAnn's room," he said, as if that explained it.

"Your little girl?"

He nodded. "The younger of my two girls. Jane's with her mother in the kitchen."

The bed was unmade; the window was open. Lake wind whispered in.

"Where's JoAnn, Bob?" I asked.

"Gone," he said. He swallowed thickly. "Look at this."

He walked to the window; pointed to a scrap of paper on the floor. I walked there, knelt. I did not pick up the greasy scrap of foolscap. I didn't have to, to read the crudely printed words there:

"Get $20,000 Ready & Waite for Word. Do Not Notify FBI or Police. Bills in 5's and 10's. Burn this for her safty!"

I stood and sucked in some air; hands on hips, I looked into Bob Keenan's wide, red, desperate eyes and said, "You haven't called the cops?"

"No. Or the FBI. I called you."

Sounding more irritable than I meant to, I said, "For Christ's sake, why?"

"The note said no police. I needed help. I may need an intermediary. I sure as hell need somebody who knows his way around this kind of thing."

I gestured with open, raised palms, like a mime making a wall. "Don't touch anything. Have you touched anything?"

"No. Not even the note."

"Good. Good." I put my hand on his shoulder. "Now, just take it easy, Bob. Let's go sit in the living room."

I walked him in there, hand never leaving his shoulder.

"Okay," I said gently, "why exactly did you call *me*?"

He was next to me on the couch, sitting slumped, staring downward, legs apart, hands clasped. He was a big man—not fat: big.

He shrugged. "I knew you worked on the Lindbergh case."

Yeah, and hadn't *that* worked out swell.

"I was a cop, then," I said. "I was the liaison between the Chicago PD and the New Jersey authorities. And that was a long time ago."

"Well, Ken mentioned it once."

"Did you call Ken before you called me? Did he suggest you call me?"

Ken was the attorney who was our mutual friend and business associate.

"No. Nate ... to be quite frank with you, I called because, well ... you're supposed to be connected."

I sighed. "I've had dealings with the Outfit from time to time, but I'm no gangster, Bob, and even if I was ..."

"I didn't mean that! If you were a gangster, do you think I would have called you?"

"I'm not understanding this, Bob."

His wife, Norma, entered the room tentatively; she was a pretty, petite woman in a floral-print dress that was like a darker version of the wallpaper in her little girl's room. Her pleasant features were distorted; there was a wildness in her face. She hadn't cried yet. She was too upset.

I stood. If I'd ever felt more awkward, I couldn't remember when.

"Is everything all right, Bob? Is this your detective friend?"

"Yes. This is Nate Heller."

She came to me and gave me a skull-like smile. "Thank for you coming. Oh, thank you so much for coming. Can you help us?"

"Yes," I said. It was the only thing I could say.

Relief filled her chest and filtered up through her face; but her eyes remained wild.

"Please go sit with Jane," Bob said, patting her arm. He looked at me as if an explanation were necessary. "Jane and her little sister are so very close. She and JoAnn are only two years apart."

I nodded, and the wife went hurriedly away, as if rushing to make sure Jane were still there.

We sat back down.

"I know you've had dealings with the mob," Keenan said. "The problem is ... so I have I. Or actually, the problem is, I haven't."

"Pardon?"

He sighed and shook his head. "I only moved here six months ago. I'd been second-in-command in the New York office. In Albany."

"Of the OPA, you mean?"

"Yes," he said, nodding. "I guess I don't have to tell you the pressures a person in my position is under. We're in charge of everything from building and industrial materials to meat to gasoline to ... well. Anyway. I didn't play ball with the mobsters out there. There were threats against me, against my family, but I didn't take their money. I asked for a transfer. I was sent here."

Chicago? That was a hell of a place to hide from mobsters.

He read the thought in my face.

"I know," he said, raising an eyebrow, "but I wasn't given a choice in the matter. Oddly, none of that type of people have contacted me here. But then, things are winding down ... rationing's all but a thing of the past." He laughed mirthlessly. "That's the irony. The sad goddamn irony."

"What is?"

He was shaking his head. "The announcement will be made later this week: the OPA is out of business. They're shutting us down. I'm moving over to a Department of Agriculture position."

"I see." I let out another sigh; it was that kind of situation.

"So, because the note said not to notify the authorities, and because you've had threats from gangsters before, you called me in."

I had my hands on my knees; he placed his hand over my nearest one, and squeezed. It was an earnest gesture, and embarrassed hell out of me.

"You've got to help us," he said.

"I will. I will. I'll be glad to serve as an intermediary, and I'll be glad to advise you and do whatever you think will be useful."

"Thank God," he said.

"But first we call the cops."

"What ...?"

"Are you a gambling man, Bob?"

"Well, yes, I suppose, in a small way, but not with my daughter's *life*, for God's sake!"

"I know what the odds are in a case like this. In a case like this, children are recovered unharmed more frequently when the police and FBI are brought in."

"But the note said ..."

"How old is JoAnn?"

"She's six."

"That's old enough for her to be able to describe her kidnappers. That's old enough for her to pick them out of a lineup."

"I don't understand what you're saying."

"Bob." And now I reached over and clasped *his* hand. He looked at me with haunted, watery eyes. "Kidnapping's a federal offense, Bob. It's a capital crime."

He swallowed. "Then they'll probably kill her, won't they? If she isn't dead already."

"Your chances are better with the authorities in on it. We'll work it from both ends: negotiate with the kidnappers, even as the cops are beating the bushes trying to find the bastards. And JoAnn."

"If she's not already dead," he said.

I just looked at him. Then I nodded.

He began to weep.

I patted his back, gently. There there. There there.

3

The first cop to arrive was Detective Kruger from Summerdale District station; he was a stocky man in a rumpled suit with an equally rumpled face. His was the naturally mournful countenance of a hound. He looked a little more mournful than usual as he glanced around the child's bedroom.

Keenan was tagging along, pointing things out. "That window," he said, "I only had it open maybe five inches, last night, to let in the breeze. But now it's wide open."

Kruger nodded, taking it all in.

"And the bedcovers—JoAnn would never fold them back neatly like that."

Kruger looked at Keenan with eyes that were sharp in the folds of his face. "You heard nothin' unusual last night?"

Keenan flinched, almost as if embarrassed. "Well ... my wife did."

"Could I speak to her?"

"Not just yet. Not just yet."

"Bob," I said, prompting him, trying not to intrude on Kruger but wanting to be of help, "what did Norma hear?"

"She heard the neighbor's dog barking—sometime after midnight. She sat up in bed, wide awake, thought she heard JoAnn's voice. Went to JoAnn's door, listened, didn't hear anything ... and went back to bed."

Kruger nodded somberly.

"Please don't ask her about it," Keenan said. "She's blaming herself."

We all knew that was foolish of her; but we all also knew there was nothing to done about it.

The Scientific Crime Detection Laboratory team arrived, as did the photographer attached to Homicide, and soon the place was swarming with suits and ties. Kruger, who I knew a little, which was why I'd asked for him specifically when I called the Summerdale station, buttonholed me.

"Look, Heller," he said pleasantly, brushing something off the shoulder of my suit coat. "I know you're a good man, but there's people on the force who think you smell."

A long time ago, I had testified against a couple of crooked cops—crooked even by Chicago standards. By my standards, even. But cops, like crooks, weren't supposed to rat each other out; and even fifteen years later that put me on a lot of shit lists.

"I'll try to stay downwind," I said.

"Good idea. When the feds show, they're not going to relish havin' a private eye on the scene, either."

"I'm only here because Bob Keenan wants me."

"I think he needs you here," Kruger said, nodding, "for his peace of mind. Just stay on the sidelines."

I nodded back.

Kruger had turned to move on, when as an afterthought he looked back and said, "Hey, uh—sorry about your pal Drury. That's a goddamn shame."

I'd worked with Bill Drury on the pickpocket detail back in the early '30s; he was that rare Chicago animal: an honest cop. He also had an obsessive hatred for the Outfit, which had gotten him in trouble. He was currently on suspension. "Let that be a lesson to you," I said cheerfully. "That's what happens to cops who do their jobs."

Kruger shrugged and shambled off, to oversee the forensic boys.

The day was a long one. The FBI arrived in all their officious glory; but they were efficient, putting a tape recorder on the phone, in case a ransom call should come in. Reporters got wind of the kidnapping, but outside the boys in blue roped off the area and were keeping them out for now—a crime lab team was making plaster impressions of footprints and probable ladder indentations under the bedroom window. A radio station crew was allowed to come in so Bob could record pleas to the kidnappers ("She's just a little girl ... please don't hurt her ... she was only wearing her pajamas, so wrap a blanket around her, please"). Beyond the fingerprinting and photos, the only real police work I witnessed was a brief interrogation of the maid of the family upstairs; a colored girl named Leona, she reported hearing JoAnn say, "I'm sleepy," around half past midnight. Leona's room was directly above the girl's.

Kruger came over and sat on the couch next to me, around lunchtime. "Want to grab a bite somewhere, Heller?"

"Sure."

He drove me to a corner café four blocks away and we sat at the counter. "We found a ladder," he said. "In a backyard a few houses to the south of Keenan's."

"Yeah? Does it match the indentations in the ground?"

Kruger nodded.

"Any scratches on the bricks near the window?"

Kruger nodded again. "Matches those, too. Ladder was a little short."

The first-floor window was seven and a half feet off the ground; the basement windows of the building were mostly exposed, in typical Chicago fashion.

"Funny thing," Kruger said. "Ladder had a broken rung."

"A broken rung? Jesus. Just like ..." I cut myself off.

"Like the Lindbergh case," Kruger said. "You worked that, didn't you?"

"Yeah."

"They killed that kid, didn't they?"

"That's the story."

"This one's dead, too, isn't she?"

The waitress came and poured us coffee.

"Probably," I said.

"Keenan thinks maybe the Outfit's behind this," Kruger said.

"I know he does."

"What do you think, Heller?"

I laughed humorlessly. "Not in a million years. This is an amateur, and a stupid one."

"Oh?"

"Who else would risk the hot seat for twenty grand?"

He considered that briefly. "You know, Heller—Keenan's made some unpopular decisions on the OPA board."

"Not unpopular enough to warrant something like this."

"I suppose." He was sugaring his coffee—overdoing it, now that sugar wasn't so scarce. His hound-dog face studied the swirling coffee as his spoon churned it up. "How do you haul a kid out of her room in the middle of the night without causing a stir?"

"I can think of two ways."

"Yeah?"

"It was somebody who knew her, and she went willingly, trustingly."

"Yeah."

"Or," I said, "they killed her in bed, and carried her out like a sack of sugar."

Kruger swallowed thickly; then he raised his coffee and sipped. "Yeah," he said.

4

I left Kruger at the counter where he was working on a big slice of apple pie, and used a pay phone to call home.

"Nate," Peg said, before I'd had a chance to say anything, "don't you know that fellow Keenan? Robert Keenan?"

"Yes," I said.

"I just heard him on the radio," she said. Her voice sounded both urgent and upset. "His daughter ..."

"I know," I said. "Bob Keenan is who called me this morning. He called me before he called the police."

There was a pause. Then: "Are you working on the case?"

"Yes. Sort of. The cops and the FBI, it's their baby." Poor choice of words. I moved ahead quickly: "But Bob wants me around. In case an intermediary is needed or something."

"Nate, you've got to help him. You've got to help him get his little girl back."

This morning was forgotten. No talk of divorce now. Just a pregnant mother frightened by the radio, wanting some reassurance from her man. Wanting him to tell her that this glorious post-war world really was a wonderful, safe place to bring a child into.

"I'll try, Peg. I'll try. Don't wait supper for me."

That afternoon, a pair of plainclothes men gave Kruger a sobering report. They stayed out of Keenan's earshot, but Kruger didn't seem to mind my eavesdropping.

They—and several dozen more plainclothes dicks—had been combing the neighborhood, talking to neighbors and specifically to the janitors of the many apartment buildings in the area. One of these janitors had found something disturbing in his basement laundry room.

"Blood smears in a laundry tub," a thin young detective told Kruger.

"And a storage locker that had been broken into," his older, but just as skinny partner said. "Some shopping bags scattered around—and some rags that were stained, too. Reddish-brown stains."

Kruger stared at the floor. "Let's get a forensic team over there."

The detectives nodded, and went off to do that.

Mrs. Keenan and ten-year-old Jane were upstairs, at the neighbors', through all of this; but Bob stayed right there, at the phone, waiting for it to ring. It didn't.

I stayed pretty close to him, though I circulated from time to time, picking up on what the detectives were saying. The mood was grim. I drank a lot of coffee, till I started feeling jumpy, then backed off.

Late afternoon, Kruger caught my eye and I went over to him.

"That basement with the laundry tubs," he said quietly. "In one of the drains, there were traces of blood, chips of bone, fragments of flesh, little clumps of hair."

"Oh God."

"I'm advising Chief of Detectives Storms to send teams out looking."

"Looking for what?"

"What do you think?"

"God."

"Heller, I want to get started right now. I can use you. Give Keenan some excuse."

I went over to Bob, who sat on the edge of a straight-backed chair by the phone stand. His glazed eyes were fixed on the phone.

"I'm going to run home for supper," I told him. "Little woman's in the family way, you know, and I got to check in with her or get in dutch. Can you hold down the fort?"

"Sure, Nate. Sure. You'll come back, though?"

I patted his shoulder. "I'll come right back."

Kruger and I paired up; half a dozen other teams, made up of plainclothes and uniformed men already at the scene, went out into the field as well. More were on the way. We were to look under every porch, behind every bush, in every basement, in every coal bin, trash can, any possible hiding place where a little body—or what was left of one—might be stowed.

"We'll check the sewers, too," Kruger said, as we walked down the sidewalk. It was dusk now; the streetlamps had just come on. Coolness off the lake helped you forget it was July. The city seemed washed in gray-blue, but night hadn't stolen away the clarity of day.

I kept lifting manhole covers and Kruger would cast the beam of his flashlight down inside, but we saw nothing but muck.

"Let's not forget the catch basins," I said.

"Good point."

We began checking those as well, and in the passageway between two brick apartment buildings directly across from the similar building that housed those bloody laundry tubs, the circular iron catch-basin lid—like a manhole cover, but smaller—looked loose.

"Somebody opened that recently," Kruger said. His voice was quiet but the words were ominous in the stillness of the darkening night.

"We need something to pry it up a little," I said, kneeling. "Can't get my fingers under it."

"Here," Kruger said. He plucked the badge off the breast pocket of his jacket and, bending down, used the point of the star to pry the lid up to where I could wedge my fingers under it.

I slid the heavy iron cover away, and Kruger tossed the beam of the flashlight into the hole.

A face looked up at us.

A child's face, framed in blonde, muck-dampened, darkened hair.

"It looks like a doll," Kruger said. He sounded out of breath.

"That's no doll," I said, and backed away, knowing I'd done as my wife had requested: I'd found Bob Keenan's little girl.

Part of her, anyway.

We fished the little head out of the sewer; how, exactly, I'd rather not go into. It involved the handle of a broom we borrowed from the janitor of one of the adjacent buildings.

Afterward, I leaned against the bricks in the alleylike passageway, my back turned away from what we'd found. Kruger tapped me on the shoulder.

"You all right, Heller?"

Uniformed men were guarding the head, which rested on some newspapers we'd spread out on the cement near the catch basin; they were staring down at it like it was some bizarre artifact of a primitive culture.

"About lost my lunch," I said.

"You're white as an Irishman's ass."

"I'm okay."

Kruger lighted up a cigarette; its amber eye glowed.

"Got another of those?" I asked.

"Sure." He got out a deck of Lucky Strikes. Shook one out for me. I took it hungrily and he thumbed a flame on his Zippo and lit me up. "Never saw you smoke before, Heller."

"Hardly ever do. I used to, overseas. Everybody did, over there."

"I bet. You were on Guadalcanal, I hear."

"Yeah."

"Pretty rough?"

"I thought so till tonight."

He nodded. "I made a call. Keenan's assistant, guy that runs the ration board, he's on his way. To make the ID. Can't put the father through that shit."

"You're thinking, Kruger," I said, sucking on the cigarette. "You're all right."

He grunted noncommittally and went over to greet various cops, uniform and plainclothes, who were arriving; I stayed off to one side, back to the brick wall, smoking my cigarette.

The janitor we'd borrowed the broom from sought me out. He was a thick-necked, white-haired guy in his early fifties; he wore coveralls over a flannel shirt rolled up at the sleeves.

"So sad," he said. His face was as German as his accent.

"What's on your mind, pop?"

"I saw something."

"Oh?"

"Maybe is not important."

I called Lt. Kruger over, to let him decide.

"About five this morning," the bull-necked janitor said, "I put out some trash. I see man in brown raincoat walking. His

22

head, it was down, inside his collar, like it was cold outside, only it was not cold and not raining, either. He carry shopping bag."

Kruger and I exchanged sharp glances.

"Where did you see this man walking, exactly?" Kruger asked the janitor.

The stocky Kraut led us into the street; he pointed diagonally—right at the brick mansion where the Keenans lived. "He cut across that lawn, and walk west."

"What's your name, pop?" I asked.

"Otto. Otto Bergstrum."

Kruger gave Otto the janitor over to a pair of plainclothes dicks and they escorted him off to Summerdale District station to take a formal statement.

"Could be a break," Kruger said.

"Could be," I said.

Keenan's OPA coworker, Walter Munsen, a heavyset fellow in his late forties, was allowed through the wall of blue uniforms to look at the chubby-cheeked head on the spread-out papers. It looked up at him, its sweet face nicked with cuts, its neck a ragged thing. He said, "Sweet Jesus. That's her. That's little JoAnn."

That was good enough for Kruger.

We walked back to the Keenan place. A starless, moonless night had settled on the city, as if God wanted to blot out what man had done. It didn't work. The flashing red lights of squad cars, and the beams of cars belonging to the morbidly curious, fought the darkness. Reporters and neighbors infested the sidewalks in front of the Keenan place. Word of our grim discovery had spread—but not to Keenan himself.

At the front door, Kruger said, "I'd like you to break it to him, Heller."

"Me? Why the hell me?"

"You're his friend. You're who he called. He'll take it better from you."

"Bullshit. There's no 'better' *in* this."

But I did the deed.

We stood in one corner of the living room. Kruger was at my side, but I did the talking. Keenan's wife was still upstairs at the neighbors. I put a hand on his shoulder and said, "It's not good, Bob."

He already knew from my face. Still, he had to say: "Is she dead?" Then he answered his own question: "You've found her, and she's dead."

I nodded.

"Dear lord. Dear lord." He dropped to one knee, as if praying; but he wasn't.

I braced his shoulder. He seemed to want to get back on his feet, so I helped him do that.

He stood there with his head hung and said, "Let me tell JoAnn's mother myself."

"Bob—there's more."

"More? How can there be more?"

"I said it was bad. After she was killed, whoever did it disposed of her body by ..." God! What words were there to say this? How do you cushion a goddamn fucking blow like this?

"Nate? What, Nate?"

"She was dismembered, Bob."

"Dismembered ...?"

Better me than some reporter. "I found her head in a sewer catch basin about a block from here."

He just looked at me, eyes white all around; shaking his head, trying to make sense of the words.

Then he turned and faced the wall; hands in his pockets.

"Don't tell Norma," he said, finally.

"We have to tell her," Kruger said, as kindly as he could. "She's going to hear soon enough."

He turned and looked at me; his face was streaked with tears. "I mean ... don't tell her about ... the ... dismembering part."

"Somebody's got to tell her," Kruger insisted.

"Call their parish priest," I told Kruger, and he bobbed his dour hound-dog head.

The priest—Father O'Shea of St. Gertrude's church—arrived just as Mrs. Keenan was being ushered back into her apartment. Keenan took his wife by the arm and walked her to the sofa; she was looking at her silent husband's tragic countenance with alarm.

The priest, a little white-haired fellow with Bible and rosary in hand, said, "How strong is your faith, my child?"

Keenan was sitting next to her; he squeezed her hand, and she looked up with clear eyes, but her lips were trembling. "My faith is strong, father."

The priest paused, trying to find the words. I knew the feeling.

"Is she all right, father?" Norma Keenan asked. The last vestiges of hope clung to the question.

The priest shook his head no.

"Is ... is she hurt?"

The priest shook his head no.

Norma Keenan knew what that meant. She stared at nothing for several long moments. Then she looked up again, but the eyes were cloudy now. "Did they ..." She began again. "Was she ... disfigured?"

The priest swallowed.

I said, "No she wasn't, Mrs. Keenan."

Somebody had to have the decency to lie to the woman.

"Thank God," Norma Keenan said. "Thank God."

She began to sob, and her husband hugged her desperately.

5

Just before ten that night, a plainclothes team found JoAnn's left leg in another catch basin. Less than half an hour later, the same team checked a manhole nearby and found her right leg in a shopping bag.

Not long after, the torso turned up—in a sewer gutter, bundled in a fifty-pound cloth sugar bag.

Word of these discoveries rocketed back to the Keenan apartment, which had begun to fill with mucky-mucks—the Police Commissioner, the Chief of Detectives and his Deputy Chief, the head of the homicide detail, the Coroner and, briefly, the Mayor. The State's Attorney and his right-hand investigator, Captain Daniel "Tubbo" Gilbert, came and stayed.

The big shots showing didn't surprise me, with a headline-bound crime like this. But the arrival of Tubbo Gilbert, who was Outfit all the way, was unsettling—considering Bob Keenan's early concerns about mob involvement.

"Heller," well-dressed Tubbo said amiably, "what rock did you crawl out from under?"

Tubbo looked exactly like his name sounded.

"Excuse me," I said, and brushed past him.

It was time for me to fade.

I went to Bob to say my good-byes. He was seated on the couch, talking to several FBI men; his wife was upstairs, at the neighbors again, under sedation.

"Nate," Keenan said, standing, patting the air with one hand, his bloodshot eyes beseeching me, "before you go ... I need a word. Please."

"Sure."

We ducked into the bathroom. He shut the door. My eyes caught a child's yellow rubber duck on the edge of the claw-footed tub.

"I want you to stay on the job," Keenan said.

"Bob, every cop in town is going to be on this case. The last thing you need, or they want, is a private detective in the way."

"Did you see who was out there?"

"A lot of people. Some very good people, mostly."

"That fellow Tubbo Gilbert. I know about him. I was warned about him. They call him 'the Richest Cop in Chicago,' don't they?"

"That's true." And that was saying something, in Chicago.

Keenan's eyes narrowed. "He's in with the gangsters."

"He's in with a lot of people, Bob, but ..."

"I'll write you a check ..." And he withdrew a checkbook from his pants pocket and knelt at the toilet and began filling a check out, frantically, using the lid as a writing table.

This was as embarrassing as it was sad. "Bob ... please don't do this ..."

He stood and handed me a check for one thousand dollars. The ink glistened wetly.

"It's a retainer," he said. "All I want from you is to keep an eye on the case. Keep these Chicago cops honest."

That was a contradiction of terms, but I let it pass.

"Okay," I said, and folded the check up and slipped it in my pocket, smearing the ink, probably. I didn't think I'd be keeping it, but the best thing to do right now was just take it.

He pumped my hand and his smile was an awful thing. "Thank you, Nate. God bless you, Nate. Thank you for everything, Nate."

We exited the bathroom and everybody eyed us strangely, as if wondering if we were perverts. Many of these cops didn't like me much, and were glad to see me go.

Outside, several reporters recognized me and called out. I ignored them as I moved toward my parked Plymouth; I hoped I wasn't blocked in. Hal Davis of the *News*, a small man with a big head, bright-eyed and boyish despite his fifty-some years, tagged along.

"You want to make an easy C-note?" Davis said.

"Why I'm fine, Hal. How are you?"

"I hear you were the one that fished the kid's noggin outa the shit soup."

"That's touching, Hal. Sometimes I wonder why you haven't won a Pulitzer yet, with your way with words."

"I want the exclusive interview."

I walked faster. "Fuck you."

"Two C's."

I stopped. "Five."

"Christ! Success has gone to your head, Heller."

"I might do better elsewhere. What's the hell's that all about?"

In the alley behind the Keenan house, some cops were holding reporters back while a crime-scene photographer faced a wooden fence, flashbulbs popping, making little explosions in the night.

"Damned if I know," Davis said, and was right behind me as I moved quickly closer.

The cops kept us back, but we could see it, all right. Written on the fence, in crude red lettering, were the words: "Stop me before I kill more."

"Jesus Christ," Davis said, all banjo-eyed. "Is *that* who did this? The goddamn *Lipstick* Killer?"

"The Lipstick Killer," I repeated numbly.

Was that who did this?

6

The Lipstick Killer, as the press had termed him, had hit the headlines for the first time last January.

Mrs. Caroline Williams, an attractive forty-year-old widow with a somewhat shady past, was found nude and dead in bed in her modest North Side apartment. A red skirt and a nylon stocking were tied tightly around the throat of the voluptuous brunette corpse. There had been a struggle, apparently—the room was topsy-turvy. Mrs. Williams had been beaten, her face bruised, battered.

She'd bled to death from a slashed throat, and the bed was soaked red; but she was oddly clean. Underneath the tightly tied red dress and nylon, the coroner found an adhesive bandage over the neck wound.

The tub in the bathroom was filled with bloody water and the victim's clothing, as if wash were soaking.

A suspect—an armed robber who was the widow's latest gentleman friend—was promptly cleared. Caroline Williams had been married three times, leaving two divorced husbands and one dead one. Her ex-husbands had unshakable alibis, particularly the latter.

The case faded from the papers, and dead-ended for the cops.

Then just a little over a month ago, a similar crime—apparently, even obviously, committed by the same hand—had rattled the city's cage. Mrs. Williams, who'd gotten around after all, had seemed the victim of a crime of passion. But when Margaret Johnson met a disturbingly similar fate, Chicago knew it had a madman at large.

Margaret Johnson—her friends called her Peggy (my wife's nickname)—was twenty-nine years old and a beauty. A well-liked, churchgoing small-town girl, she'd just completed three years of war service with the Waves to go to work in the office of a business machine company in the Loop. She was found nude and dead in her small flat in a North Side residential hotel.

When a hotel maid found her, Miss Johnson was slumped, kneeling, at the bathtub, head over the tub. Her hair was wrapped turbanlike in a towel, her pajama top tied loosely around her neck, through which a bread knife had been driven with enough force to go in one side and poke out the other.

She'd also been shot—once in the head, again in the arm. Her palms were cut, presumably from trying to wrest the knife from the killer's hand.

The blood had been washed from the ex-Wave's body. Damp, bloody towels were scattered about the bathroom floor. The outer room of the small apartment was a shambles, bloodstains everywhere. Most significantly, fairly high up on the wall, in letters three to six inches tall, printed in red with the victim's lipstick, were the words:

> For heavens
> Sake catch me
> Before I Kill More
> I cannot control myself.

The cops and the papers called the Lipstick Killer (the nickname was immediate) a "sex maniac," though neither woman had been raped. The certainty of the police in that characterization made me suspicious that something meaningful had been withheld.

I had asked Lt. Bill Drury, who before his suspension had worked the case out of Town Hall Station, and he said semen had been found on the floor in both apartments, near the windows that had apparently given the killer entry in either flat.

What we had here was a guy who needed one hell of a visual aid to jack off.

What these two slain women had in common with the poor butchered little JoAnn Keenan, I wasn't sure, other than violent death at the hands of a madman with something sharp; the body parts of the child were largely drained of blood. That was about it.

But the lipstick message on that alley fence—even down to the childlike lettering—would serve to fuel the fires of this investigation even further. The papers had already been calling the Lipstick Killer "Chicago's Jack the Ripper." With the slaying of the kidnapped girl, the city would undoubtedly go off the deep end.

"The papers have been riding the cops for months," I told my Peg that night, as we cuddled in bed; she was trembling in the hollow of my arm. "Calling them Keystone Kops, ridiculing the ineffectiveness of their crime lab work. And their failure to nab the Lipstick Killer has been a club the papers've beat 'em with."

"You sound like you think that's unfair," Peg said.

"I do, actually. A lunatic can be a lot harder to catch than a career criminal. And this guy's MO is all over the map."

"MO?"

"The way he does his crimes, the kind of crimes he does. Even the two women he killed, there are significant differences. The second was shot, and that, despite the knife through the throat, was the cause of death. Is it okay if I talk about this?"

She nodded. She was a tough cookie.

"Anyway," I went on, "the guy hasn't left a single workable fingerprint."

"Cleans up after himself," she said.

"Half fetish," I said, "half cautious."

"Completely nuts."

"Completely nuts," I agreed. I smiled at her. It was dark in the bedroom, but I could see her sweet face, staring into nothing.

Quietly, she said, "You told your friend Bob Keenan that you'd stay on the job."

"Yeah. I was just pacifying him."

"You *should* stay on it."

"I don't know if I can. The cops, hell the feds, they're not exactly going to line up for my help."

"Since when does that kind of thing stop you? Keep on it. You've got to find this fiend." She took my hand and placed it on her full tummy. "Got to."

"Sure, Peg. Sure."

I gave her tummy the same sort of "there there" pat I'd given Bob Keenan's shoulder. And I felt a strange, sick gratefulness to the Lipstick Killer, suddenly: the day had begun with my wife asking for a divorce.

It had ended with me holding her, comforting her.

In this glorious post-war world, I'd take what I could get.

7

Two days later, I was treating my friend Bill Drury to lunch in that bustling Loop landmark of a restaurant, the Berghoff. Waiters in tuxes, steaming platters of food lifted high, threaded around tables like runners on some absurd obstacle course. The patrons—mostly businessmen, though a few lady shoppers and matinee-goers were mixed in—created a din of chatter and clinking tableware that made every conversation in this wide-open space a private one.

Bill liked to eat, and had accepted my invitation eagerly, even though it had meant driving in from his home on the North Side. Even out of work, he was nattily dressed—dark blue vested suit with wide orange tie with a jeweled stickpin. His jaw jutted, his eyes were dark and sharp, his shoulders broad, his carriage intimidating. Only a pouchiness under his eyes and a touch of gray in his dark, thinning hair revealed the stress of recent months.

"I'm goddamn glad you beat the indictment," I said.

He shrugged, buttered up a slice of rye; our Wiener Schnitzel was on the way. "There's still this Grand Jury thing to deal with."

"You'll beat it," I said, but I wasn't so sure. Bill had, in his zeal to nail certain Outfit guys, paid at least one witness to testify. I'd been there when the deal was struck.

"In the meantime," he said cheerfully, "I sit twiddling my thumbs at the old homestead, making the little woman nervous with my unemployed presence."

"You want to do a little work for A-1?"

He shook his head, frowned regretfully. "I'm still a cop, Nate, suspended or not."

"It'd be just between us girls. You still got friends at Town Hall Station, don't you?"

"Of course."

A waiter old enough to be our father, and looking stern enough to want to spank us, delivered our steaming platters of veal and German fried potatoes and red cabbage.

"I'm working the Keenan case," I said, sipping my beer.

"Still? I figured you'd have dropped out by now." He snorted a laugh. "My brother says you picked up a pretty penny for that interview."

His brother John worked for the *News*.

"Davis met my price," I shrugged. "Look, Bob Keenan seems to want me aboard. Makes him feel better. Anyway, I just intend to work the fringes."

He was giving me his detective look. "That ten grand reward the *Trib* posted wouldn't have anything to do with your decision to stick, would it?"

I smiled and cut my veal. "Maybe. You interested?"

"What can *I* do?"

"First of all, you can clue me in if any of your cop buddies over at Town Hall see any political strings being pulled, or any Outfit strings, either."

He nodded and shrugged, as he chewed; that meant yes.

"Second, you worked the Lipstick killings."

"But I got yanked off, in the middle of the second."

"So play some catch-up ball. Go talk to your buddies. Sort through the files. See if something's slipped through the cracks."

His expression was skeptical. "Every cop in town is on this thing, like ugly on a monkey. What makes you think either one of us can find something *they'd* miss?"

"Bill," I said pleasantly, eating my red cabbage, "we're better detectives than they are."

"True," he said. He cut some more veal. "Anyway, I think they're going down the wrong road."

"Yeah?"

He shrugged a little. "They're focusing on sex offenders; violent criminals. But look at the MO. What do you make of it? Who would *you* look for, Nate?"

I'd thought about that a lot. I had an answer ready: "A second-story man. A cat burglar who wasn't stealing for the dough he could find, or the goods he could fence, not primarily. But for the kicks."

Drury looked at me with shrewd, narrowed eyes. "For the kicks. Exactly."

"Maybe a kid. A JD, or a JD who's getting just a little older, into his twenties maybe."

"Why do you say that?"

"Thrill-seeking is a young-at-heart kind of thing, Bill. And getting in the Johnson woman's apartment took crawling onto a narrow ledge from a fire escape. Took some pretty tricky, almost acrobatic skills. And some recklessness."

He held up his knife. "Plus, it takes strength to jam a bread knife through a woman's neck."

"I'll have to take your word for that. But it does add up to somebody on the young side."

He pointed the knife at me. "I was developing a list of just that kind of suspect ... only I got pulled off before I could follow up."

I'd hoped for something like this.

"Where's that list now?"

"In my field notes," Drury said. "But let me stop by Town Hall, and nose around a little. Before I give you anything. You want me to check around at Summerdale station, too? I got pals there."

"No," I said. "I already got Kruger, there. He's going to keep me in the know."

"Kruger's okay," Drury said, nodding. "But why's he cooperating with you, Nate?"

The fried potatoes were crisp and salty and fine, but I wished I'd asked for gravy. "That reward the *Trib*'s promising. Cops aren't eligible to cash in."

"Ah," Drury said, and drank some dark beer. "Which applies to me, as well."

"Sure. But that's no problem."

"I'm an honest cop, Nate."

"As honest as they come in this town. But you're human. We'll work something out, Bill, you and me."

"We'll start," Bill said, pushing his plate aside, grinning like a goof, "with dessert."

8

That night I stopped in at the funeral home on East Erie. Peg wasn't up to it—felt funny about it, since she'd never met the Keenans; so I went alone. A cop was posted to keep curiosity seekers out, but few made the attempt—the war might have been over, but the memory of personal sorrows was fresh.

The little girl lay dressed in white satin with pink flowers at her breast; you couldn't see the nicks on her face—she was even smiling, faintly. She looked sweetly asleep. She was arranged so that you couldn't tell the arms were still missing.

Norma Keenan had been told, of course, what exactly had happened to her little girl. My compassionate lie had only lessened her sorrow for that first night. Unbelievably, it had gotten worse: the coroner had announced, this afternoon, that there had been "attempted rape."

The parents wore severe black and, while family and friends stood chatting *sotto voce*, were seated to one side. Neither was crying. It wasn't that they were bearing up well: it was shock.

"Thanks for coming, Nate," Bob said, rising, and squeezed my hand. "Will you come to the Mass tomorrow?"

"Sure," I said. It had been a long time since I'd been to Mass; my mother had been Catholic, but she died when I was young.

At St. Gertrude's the next morning, it turned out not to be a Requiem Mass, but the Mass of the Angels, as sung by the one hundred tender voices of the children's choir. "A song of welcome," the priest said, "admitting another to sing before the throne of God."

JoAnn had belonged to this choir; last Christmas, she'd played an angel in the Scared Heart school pageant.

Now she was an armless corpse in a casket at the altar rail; even the beauty of the children's voices and faces, even the long, tapering white candles that cast a flickery golden glow on the little white coffin, couldn't erase that from my mind. When the priest reminded those in attendance that "there is no room for vengeance in our hearts," I bit my tongue. *Speak for yourself, padre.*

People wept openly, men and women alike, many hugging their own children. Some thirteen hundred had turned out for the Mass; a detail of policemen protected the Keenans as they exited the church. The crowd, however, was well behaved.

And only a handful of us were at the cemetery. The afternoon was overcast, unseasonably chilly, and the wind coursed through All Saints' like a guilty conscience. After a last blessing of holy water from the priest, the little white casket was lowered into a tiny grave protected by a solitary maple. Flowers banking the grave fluttered and danced in the breeze.

I didn't allow myself to cry, not at first. I told myself Keenan was an acquaintance, not a friend; I reminded myself that I had never met the little girl—not before I fished her head out of a goddamn sewer, anyway. I held back the tears, and was a man.

It wasn't till I got home that night, and saw my pregnant wife, that it hit me; knocked the slats right out from under me.

Then I found myself sitting on the couch, crying like a baby, and this time she was comforting me.

It didn't last long, but when it stopped, I came to a strange and disturbing realization: everything I'd been through in this life, from close calls as a cop to fighting Japs in the Pacific, hadn't prepared me for fear like this. For the terror of being a parent. Of knowing something on the planet was so precious to you the very thought of losing it invited madness.

"You're going to help your friend," Peg said. "You're going to get whoever did this."

"I'm going to try, baby," I said, rubbing the wetness away with the knuckles of one hand. "Hell, the combined rewards are up to thirty-six grand."

9

The next day, however, I did little on the Keenan case. I did check in with both Kruger and Drury, neither of whom had much for me—nothing that the papers hadn't already told me.

Two janitors had been questioned, and considered suspects, briefly. One of them was the old Kraut we'd borrowed the broomstick from—Otto Bergstrum. The other was an Army vet in his early twenties named James Watson, who was the handyman for the nursery from which the kidnap ladder had been stolen. Watson was a prime suspect because, as a juvenile offender, he'd been arrested for molesting an eight-year-old girl.

That long-ago charge had been knocked down to disorderly conduct, however, and meanwhile, back in the present, both Bergstrum and Watson had alibis. Also, they both passed lie-detector tests.

"It doesn't look like there's any significance," Kruger told me on the phone, "to that locker the killer broke into."

"In the so-called 'murder cellar,' you mean?"

"Yeah. Kidnapper stole rags and shopping bags out of it. The guy's clean, whose locker that is."

"Any good prints turn up?"

"No. Not in the murder cellar, or the girl's room. We had two on the window that turned out to be the cleaning lady. We do have a crummy partial off the kidnap note. And we have some picture-frame wire, a loop of it, we found in an alley near

42

the Keenan house; might've been used to strangle the girl. The coroner says she was dead before she was cut up."

"Thank God for that much."

"We have a couple of odd auto sightings, near the Keenan house, in the night and early morning. We're looking into that."

"A car makes sense," I said. "Otherwise, you'd think somebody would've spotted this maniac hand-carrying the body from the Keenans' over to that basement."

"I agree. But it was the middle of the night. Time of death, after all, was between one thirty and two a.m."

Kruger said he'd keep me posted, and that had been that, for me and the Keenan case, on that particular day.

With one rather major exception.

I was about to get into my Plymouth, in a parking garage near the Rookery, when a dark blue 1946 Mercury slid up and blocked me in.

Before I had the chance to complain, the driver looked out at me and grinned. "Let's take a spin, Heller."

He was a thin-faced, long-chinned, beak-nosed, gray-complected guy about forty; he wasn't big, but his presence was commanding. His name was Sam Flood, and he was a fast-rising Outfit guy, currently Tony Accardo's chauffeur/bodyguard. He was also called "Mooney," which was West Side street slang for nuts.

"A 'spin,' Sam—or a 'ride'?"

Sam laughed. "Come on, Heller. I got a proposition for you. Since when do you turn your nose up at dough?"

I wasn't armed, but it was cinch Flood was. Flood was a West Side boy, like me, only I grew up around Maxwell Street while he was from the Near West Side's notorious "Patch," and a veteran of the infamous street gang, the 42s.

"Let's talk right here, Sam," I said. "Nobody's around."

He thought about that; his dark eyes glittered. He pretended to like me, but I knew he didn't. He hated all cops, including ex-cops. And my status with the Outfit largely had to do with my one-time friendship with the late Frank Nitti, whom Sam had no particular respect for. Sam was, after all, a protégé of Paul Ricca, who had forced Nitti out.

"Okay," Sam said. He spoke softly, and almost haltingly. "I'm gonna park it right over there in that space. You come sit and talk. Nothing bad's gonna happen to you in my own fuckin' car."

So we sat and talked.

Sam, wearing a dark well-tailored suit and a kelly-green snap-brim, half-turned to look at me. "You know who speaks well of you?"

"Who?"

"Louie Campagna." He thumbed his chest. "I kept an eye on his missus for him while he was in stir on the movie-union rap."

"Louie's all right," I said politely. Campagna had been Nitti's right arm; for some reason, Sam wanted to reassure me that we were pals. Or at least, had mutual pals. Back in '44, I'd encountered Sam for the first time when Outfit treasurer Jake Guzik got kidnapped and I was pulled in as a neutral go-between. From that experience I had learned Sam "Mooney" Flood was one ruthless fucker, and as manipulative as a carnival barker.

"You're on this Keenan case," he said.

That would've tensed me right there, only I was already wound tight.

"Yeah," I said casually. "Not in a big way. The father's a friend, and he wants somebody to keep the cops honest."

That made him laugh. Whether it was the idea of *me* keeping somebody honest, or anybody keeping the cops honest, he didn't say.

I decided to test the waters. "You know why Keenan called me in, don't you?"

"No," Sam said. It seemed a genuine enough response.

"He was afraid the kidnapping might have been the mob getting back at him for not playing ball back east. You know, in his OPA job."

Sam nodded, but then shook his head, no. "That's not likely, Heller. The eastern mobs don't make a play on our turf without checking first."

I nodded; that made sense.

"But just so you know—if you don't already—up to very recent, I was in the gas and food stamp business."

I *had* known that, which was why seeing the little hood show up on my figurative doorstep was so chilling; not that meeting with Sam Flood would warm me up under any circumstances.

"But that's over," Sam said. "In fact, it's been over for a couple months. That racket's gone the way of speakeasies. And Heller—when we was in that business, I never, and to my knowledge, no Outfit guy never made no approach to that Keenan guy."

"He never said you did."

The gaunt face relaxed. "Good. Now—let me explain my interest in this case."

"Please do."

"It's looking like that fucking Lipstick Killer did this awful crime on this little child."

"Looks like. But some people think a crank might've written that lipstick message in the alley."

His eyes tightened. "I hear the family received a lipstick letter, too, with the same message: 'Stop me before I kill more' or whatever."

"That's true."

He sighed. Then he looked at me sharply. "Does attorney/client privilege apply to you and me, if I give you a retainer?"

"Yeah. I'd have to send you a contract with an attorney I work with, to keep it legal. Or we could do it through your attorney. But I don't know that I want you as a client, Sam. No offense."

He raised a finger. "I promise you that working for me will in no way compromise you or put you in conflict of interest with your other client, the Keenan father. If I'm lying, then the deal's off."

I said nothing.

He thrust a fat, sealed envelope into my lap. "That's a grand in fifties."

"Sam, I ..."

"I'm your client now, Heller. Got that?"

"Well ..."

"Got it?"

I swallowed and nodded. I slipped the envelope in my inside suit coat pocket.

"The Lipstick Killer," Sam said, getting us back on the track. "The first victim was a Mrs. Caroline Williams."

I nodded.

He thrust his finger in my face; I looked at it, feeling my eyes cross. It was like looking into a gun barrel. "No one, Heller, no one must know about this." The finger withdrew and the ferretlike gangster sighed and looked out the windshield at the cement wall beyond. "I have a family. Little girls. Got to protect them. Are you a father, Heller?"

"My wife's expecting."

Sam grinned. "That's great! That's wonderful." Then the grin disappeared. "Look, I'd do anything to protect my Angeline. Some guys, they flaunt their other women. Me, far as my family knows, I never strayed. Never. But ... you're a man—you understand the needs of a man."

I was starting to get the picture; or at least part of it.

"The thing is, I was seeing this woman, this Caroline Williams. For the most part, it was pretty discreet."

It must have been, if Bill Drury hadn't found out about it; he'd been on that case, after all, and his hate-on for the Outfit was legendary.

As if reading my mind, Sam said, "Not a word to your pal Drury about this! Christ. That guy's nuts."

Mooney should know.

"Anyway, there was this photo of us together. Her and me, together. I want it back."

"Not for sentimental reasons, either."

"No," he admitted frankly. "It crushed me that my friend Mrs. Williams had the bad luck to be this maniac's victim. But from what I hear, this guy was not just a sex killer. He was some kind of weirdie second-story man."

"I think so," I said. "I think he was a burglar with a hobby."

"The police reports indicated that stuff was missing. Undergarments, various personal effects. Anyway, even with Drury on the case, I was able to find out that the picture album she had the photo in wasn't among her effects."

"Maybe her family got it."

"I checked that out myself—discreetly."

"Then you think ... the killer took the photo album?"

Sam nodded. "Yeah. She had photos of herself in bathing suits and shit. If he took her underwear with him, he could've taken that, too."

"So what do you want from me?"

He looked at me hard; he clutched my arm. "All I want is that photo album. Not even that—just that one photo. It was taken in a restaurant, by one of them photo girls who come around."

"How I am supposed to find it?"

"You may find this guy before the cops do. Or, you're tight enough with the cops on the case to maybe get to it before they do. The photo album, I mean. It would embarrass me to have that come out. It would open up an ugly can of worms, and it wouldn't have nothing to do with nothing, where these crackpot killings are concerned. It would hurt me and my family and at the same time only muddy up the waters, where the case against the maniac is concerned."

I thought about that. I had to agree.

"So all you want," I said, "is that photo."

"And your discretion."

"You'd be protected," I said. "It would be through an attorney, after all. You'd be his client and he would be my client. I couldn't say a word if I wanted to."

"You'll take the job?"

"I already took your money. But what if I don't get results?"

"You keep the retainer. You find and return that picture, you get another four grand."

"What I really want," I said, "is that little girl's murderer. I want to kill that son of a bitch."

"Have all the fun you want," Sam said. "But get me my picture back."

10

Lou Sapperstein, who had once been my boss on the pickpocket detail, was the first man I added when the A-1 expanded. Pushing sixty, Lou had the hard muscular build of a linebacker and the tortoiseshell glasses and bald pate of a scholar; in fact, he was a little of both.

He leaned a palm on my desk in my office. As usual, he was in rolled-up shirtsleeves, his tie loose around his collar. "I spent all morning in the *Trib* morgue—went back a full year."

I had asked Lou to check on any breaking-and-entering cases involving assault on women. It had occurred to me that if, as Drury and I theorized, the Lipstick Killer was a cat burglar whose thrill-seeking had escalated to murder, there may have been an intermediate stage, between bloodless break-ins and homicidal ones.

"There are several possibilities," Lou said, "but one jumped right out at me ..."

He handed me a sheet torn from a spiral pad.

"Katherine Reynolds," I read aloud. Then I read the rest to myself, and said, "Some interesting wrinkles here."

Lou nodded. "Some real similarities. And it happened right smack in between killings number one and two. You think the cops have picked up on it?"

"I doubt it," I said. "This happened on the South Side. The two women who were killed were both on the North Side."

"The little girl, too."

To Chicago cops, such geographic boundaries were inviolate—a North Side case was a North Side case and a crime that happened on the South Side might as well have happened on the moon. Unfortunately, crooks didn't always think that way.

So, late that afternoon, I found myself knocking at the door of the top-floor flat of an eight-story apartment building on the South Side, near the University of Chicago. The building had once been a nurse's dormitory—Billings Hospital was nearby—and most of the residents here still were women in the mercy business.

Like Katherine Reynolds, who was wearing crisp nurse's whites, cap included, when she answered the door.

"Thanks for seeing me on such short notice, Miss Reynolds," I said, as she showed me in.

I'd caught her at the hospital, by phone, and she'd agreed to meet me here at home; she was just getting off.

"Hope I'm not interfering with your supper," I added, hat in hand.

"Not at all, Mr. Heller," she said, unpinning her nurse's cap. "Haven't even started it yet."

She was maybe thirty, a striking brunette, with her hair chopped off in a boyish cut with pageboy bangs; her eyes were large and brown and luminous, her nose pug, her teeth white and slightly, cutely bucked. Her lips were full and scarlet with lipstick. She was slender but nicely curved and just about perfect, except for a slight medicinal smell.

We sat in the living room of the surprisingly large apartment; the furnishings were not new, but they were nice. On the end table next to the couch, where we sat, was a hand-tinted color photographic portrait of a marine in dress blues, a grinning lantern-jawed young man who looked handsome and dim.

She crossed her legs and the nylons swished. I was a married man, a professional investigator here on business, and her comeliness had no effect on me whatsoever. I put my hat over my hard-on.

"Nice place you got here," I said. "Whole floor, isn't it?"

"Yes," she said. She smiled meaninglessly. "My sister and another girl, both nurses, share it with me. I think this was the head nurse's quarters, back when it was a dorm. All the other flats are rather tiny."

"How long ago was the incident?"

This was one of many questions I'd be asking her that I already knew the answer to.

"You mean the assault?" she said crisply, lighting a cigarette up. She exhaled smoke; her lips made a glistening red O. "About four months ago. The son of a bitch came in through the skylight." She gestured to it. "It must have been around seven a.m. Sis and Dottie were already at work, so I was alone here. I was still asleep ... actually, just waking up."

"Or did something wake you up?"

"That may have been it. I half-opened my eyes, saw a shadowy figure, and then something crashed into my head." She touched her brown boyish hair. "Fractured my skull. I usually wear my hair longer, you know, but they cut a lot of it off."

"Looks good short. Do you know what you were hit with?"

"Your classic blunt instrument. I'd guess, a lead pipe. I took a good knock."

"You were unconscious."

"Oh yes. When I woke up, on the floor by the bed, maybe forty minutes later, blood was streaming down my face, and into my eyes. Some of it was sticky, already drying. My apartment was all out of kilter. Virtually ransacked. My hands were tied with a lamp cord, rather loosely. I worked myself free, easily. I looked around and some things were missing." She made an embarrassed face, gestured with a cigarette in hand. "Underwear. Panties. Bras. But also a hundred and fifty bucks were gone from my purse."

"Did you call the police at that point?"

"No. That's when I heard the knock at the door. I staggered over there and it was a kid—well, he could've been twenty, but I'd guess eighteen. He had dark hair, long and greased back. Kind of a good-looking kid. Like a young Cornell Wilde. Looked a little bit like a juvenile delinquent, or anyway, like a kid trying to look like one and not quite pulling it off."

"What do you mean?"

"Well, he wore a black leather jacket, and a T-shirt and dungarees ... but they looked kind of new. Too clean. More like a costume than clothing."

"What did he want?"

"He said he was a delivery boy—groceries, and he was looking for the right apartment to make his delivery."

"He was lost."

"Yes, but we didn't spend much time discussing that. He took one look at my bloody face and said he would get some help right away."

"And did he?"

She nodded; exhaled smoke again. "He found the building manager, told him the lady in the penthouse flat was injured, and needed medical attention. And left."

"And the cops thought he might have been the one who did it? Brought back by a guilty conscience?"

"Yes. But I'm not sure I buy that."

I nodded. But to me it tied in: the murderer who washed and bandaged his victims' wounds displayed a similar misguided *stop-me-catch-me* remorse. Even little JoAnn's body parts had been cleansed—before they were disposed of in sewers.

"The whole thing made me feel like a jerk," she said.

That surprised me. "Why?"

She lifted her shoulders; it did nice things to her cupcake breasts. Yes, I know. I'm a heel. "Well, if only I'd reacted quicker, I might have been able to protect myself. I mean, I've had all sorts of self-defense training."

"Oh?"

She flicked ashes into a glass tray on the couch arm. "I'm an Army nurse—on terminal leave. I served overseas. European theater."

"Ah."

She gave me a sly smile. "You were in the Pacific, weren't you?"

"Well, uh, yes."

"I read about you in the papers. I recognized your name right away. You're kind of well known around town."

"Don't believe everything you read in the papers, Miss Reynolds."

"You won the Silver Star, didn't you?"

I was getting embarrassed. I nodded.

"So did Jack."

"Jack?"

"My husband. He was a marine, too. You were on Guadalcanal?"

"Yes."

"So was Jack." She smiled. Then the smile faded and she sucked smoke in again. "Only he didn't come back."

"Lot of good men didn't. I'm sorry."

She made a dismissive gesture with a red-nailed hand. "Mr. Heller, why are you looking into this?"

"I think it may relate to another case. That's all."

"The Lipstick Killer?"

I hesitated, then nodded. "But I'd appreciate it if you didn't say anything about it to anybody just yet."

"Why haven't the cops done anything about this?"

"You mean, the Lipstick Killer, or what happened to you ...?"

"Both! And, why have *you* made this connection, when they haven't?"

I shrugged. "Maybe I'm more thorough. Or maybe I'm just grasping at straws."

"Well, it occurred to *me* there might be a connection. You'd think it would've occurred to the police, too!"

"You'd think."

"You know, there's something ... never mind."

"What?"

She shook her head, tensed her lips. "There was something ... creepy ... that I never told anybody about." She looked at me with eyes impossibly large, so dark brown the irises were lost. "But I feel like I can talk to you."

She touched my hand. Hers was warm. Mine felt cold.

"On the floor ... in the bathroom ... I found something. Something I just ... cleaned up. Didn't tell anybody about. It embarrassed me."

"You're a nurse ..."

"I know. But I was embarrassed just the same. It was ... come."

"What?"

"There was come on the floor. You know—ejaculate. Semen."

54

11

When I got home, I called Drury and told him about Katherine Reynolds.

"I think you may be on to something," Drury said. "You should tell Lt. Kruger about this."

"I'll call him tomorrow. But I wanted to give you the delivery boy's description first—see if it rang any bells."

Drury made a clicking sound. "Lot of kids in those black leather jackets these days. Don't know what the world's coming to. Lot of kids trying to act like they're in street gangs, even when they're not."

"Could he be a University of Chicago student?"

"Pulling crimes on the North Side?"

Even a cop as good as Drury wore the geographical blinders.

"Yeah," I said. "There's this incredible new mode of transportation they call the El. It's just possible our boy knows about it."

Drury ignored the sarcasm. "Lot of greasy-haired would-be underage hoods around, Nate. Doesn't really narrow the field much."

"That look like a young Cornell Wilde?"

"That want to," Drury said, "yes."

We sighed, and hung up.

Eavesdropping, Peg was half in the kitchen, half in the hall. She wore a white apron over the swell of her tummy. She'd made meat loaf. The smell of it beckoned. Despite herself, Peg was a hell of a cook.

"Good-looking?" she asked.

"What?"

"This nurse you went and talked to," she said.

"Oh. I didn't notice."

She smirked; went back into the kitchen. I followed. I waited at the table while she stirred gravy.

"Blonde?" she asked, her back to me.

"No. Brunette, I think."

She looked over her shoulder at me. "You think?"

"Brunette."

"Nice and slender, I'll bet. With a nice shape. Not fat and sloppy. Not a cow. Not an elephant."

"Peg...."

She turned; her wooden spoon dripped brown gravy onto the linoleum. "I'm going crazy out here, Nate. I'm ugly, and I'm bored."

"You're not ugly. You're beautiful."

"Fuck you, Heller! I'm an ugly cow, and I'm *bored* out here in the sticks. Jesus, couldn't we live someplace where there's somebody for me to talk to?"

"We have neighbors."

"Squirrels, woodchucks, and that dip down the street who mows his lawn on the even days and washes his car on the odd. It's all vacant lots and nurseries and prairie out here. Why couldn't we live closer to the city? I feel like I'm living in a goddamn pasture. Which is where a cow like me belongs, I suppose."

I stood. I went to her and held her. She was angry, but she let me.

She didn't look at me as she bit off the words. "You go off to the Loop and you can be a businessman and you can be a detective and you have your coworkers and your friends and contacts and interview beautiful nurses and you make the papers and you're living a real life. Not stuck out here in a box with a lawn. Listening to 'Ma Perkins.' Peeling potatoes. Ironing shirts."

"Baby ..."

She thumped her chest with a forefinger. "I used to have a life. I was a professional woman. I was an executive secretary."

"I know, I know."

"Nate—Nate, I'm afraid."

"Afraid?"

"Afraid I'm not cut out to be a housewife. Afraid I'm not cut out to be a mother."

I smiled at her gently; touched her face the same way. Touched her tummy. "You're already a mother, by definition. Give it a chance. The kid will change things. The neighborhood will grow."

"I hate it here."

"Give it a year. You don't like it, we'll move. Closer to town."

She smiled tightly, bravely. Nodded. Turned back to the stove.

The meal was good. We had apple pie, which may have been sarcasm on Peg's part, but if so it was delicious sarcasm. We chatted about business; about family. After the tension, things got relaxed.

We were cuddled on the couch listening to big band music on the radio when the phone rang. It was Drury again.

"Listen," he said, "sorry to bother you, but I've been thinking, and something did jog loose, finally."

"Swell! What?"

"There was this kid I busted a few years back. He was nice-looking, dark-haired, but kind of on the hoody side, though he had a good family. His dad was a security guard with a steel mill. Anyway, the boy was a good student, a bright kid—only for kicks, he stole. Furs, clothes, jewelry, old coins, guns."

"You were working out of Town Hall Station at the time?"

"Yeah. All his robberies were on the North Side. He was just thirteen."

"How old is he now?"

"Seventeen."

"Then this was a while ago."

"Yeah, but I busted him again, on some ten burglaries, two years ago. He's agile, Nate—something of human fly, navigating ledges, fire escapes ... going in windows."

"I see."

"Anyway, he did some time at Gibault." That was a correctional institution for boys at Terre Haute. "But supposedly he came out reformed. He's a really good student—so good, at seventeen, he's a sophomore in college."

"At the University of Chicago?" I said.

"Yeah," Drury said. "And guess what his part-time job is?"

"Delivery boy," I said.

"What a detective you are," Drury said.

Jerome Lapps, precocious seventeen-year-old sophomore science student, resided at a dormitory on the University of Chicago campus.

On the phone Drury had asked, "You know where his folks live?"

"What, you take me for a psychic?"

"You could've tripped over this kid, Nate. The Lapps family lives in Lincolnwood."

He gave me the address; not so far from Peg and me.

Sobering as that was, what was more interesting was that the kid lived at school, not home; even during summer session. Specifically, he was in Gates Hall on the Midway campus.

The Midway, a mile-long block-wide parkway between 59th and 60th, connected Washington and Jackson parks, and served to separate Hyde Park and the University eggheads from the real South Side. Just beyond the Midway were the Gothic limestone buildings and lushly landscaped acres of the university. At night the campus looked like another world. Of course, it looked like another world in the daylight, too.

But this was night, and the campus seemed largely deserted. That was partly summer, partly not. I left the Plymouth in a quadrangle parking lot and found my way to the third floor of Gates Hall, where I went to Lapps' room and knocked on the door. No answer. I knocked again. No answer. The door was locked.

A student well into his twenties—probably a vet on the GI Bill—told me where to find the grad student who was the resident assistant in charge of that floor.

The resident assistant leaned against the doorjamb of his room with a bottle of beer in his hand and his shirt half tucked in. His hair was red, his eyes hooded, his mouth smirky. He was perhaps twenty years old.

"What can I do for you, bud?" the kid asked.

"I'm Jerry Lapps' uncle. Supposed to meet him at his room, but he's not in."

"Yeah?"

"You got a key? I'd like to wait inside."

He shrugged. "Against the rules."

"I'm his uncle Abraham," I said. And I showed him a five-dollar bill. "I'm sure it'll be okay."

The redheaded kid brightened; his eyes looked almost awake. He snatched the five-spot and said, "Ah. Honest Abe. Jerry mentioned you."

He let me into Lapps' room and went away.

Judging by the pair of beds, one against either wall, Jerome Lapps had a roommate. But the large single room accommodated two occupants nicely. One side was rather spartan and neat as a boot-camp barracks, while across the room an unmade bed was next to a plaster wall decorated with pictures of baseball players and heartthrob movie actors. Each side of the room had its own writing desk, and again, one was cluttered, while the other was neat.

It didn't take long to confirm my suspicion that the messy side of the room belonged to the seventeen-year-old. Inside the calculus text on the sloppy desk, the name Jerome C. Lapps was written on the flyleaf in a cramped hand. The handwriting on a notepad, filled with doodles, looked the same; written several times, occasionally underlined, were the words: "Rogers Park."

Under Jerome C. Lapps' bed were three suitcases.

In one suitcase were half of the panties and bras in the city of Chicago.

The other suitcase brimmed with jewelry, watches, two revolvers, one automatic, and a smaller zippered pouch of some kind, like an oversize shaving kit. I unzipped it and recoiled.

It was a medical kit, including hypos, knives, and a surgical saw.

I put everything back and stood there and swallowed and tried to get the image of JoAnn Keenan's doll-like head out of my mind. The best way to do that was to get back to work, which I did, proceeding to the small closet on Jerome's side of the room. On the upper shelf I found a briefcase.

I opened it on the neater bed across the way. Inside were several thousand bucks in war bonds and postal savings certificates. He'd apparently put any cash he'd stolen into these, and any money from fenced goods, although considering that well-stuffed suitcase of jewelry and such, I couldn't imagine he'd bothered to fence much if any of what he'd taken.

As typically teenager-sloppy as his side of the dorm room was, Jerry had neatly compartmentalized his booty: ladies underwear in one bag; jewelry and watches in another; and paper goods in the briefcase. Included in the latter were clipped photos of big-shot Nazis. Hitler, Goering, and Goebbels.

Jerry had some funny fucking heroes.

Finally, in the briefcase, was a photo album. Thumbing through it, I saw photos of an attractive woman, frequently in a bathing suit and other brief, summer apparel. There was also a large photo of the same woman with a ferret-faced male friend in a nightclub setting; you could see a table of men sitting behind them as well, clearly, up a tier. A sweet and tender memento of Caroline Williams and Sam Flood's love affair.

I removed the photo, folded it without creasing it, and slipped it into my inside suit coat pocket. I put the photo album back, closed up the briefcase, and was returning it to the upper shelf of the closet when the dorm-room door opened.

"What the hell are you doing?" a male voice demanded.

I was turning around and slipping my hand under my jacket to get at my gun, at the same time, but the guy reacted fast. His hand must have hit the light switch, because the room went black and I could hear him coming at me, and then he was charging into me.

I was knocked back into the corner, by the many-paned windows, through which some light was filtering, and I saw a thin face, its teeth clenched, as the figure pressed into me and a single fist was smashing into my stomach, powerfully.

The damn guy was almost sitting on me, and I used all my strength to lift up and lift him off, heaving him bodily onto the floor. He was scrambling to his feet when I stuck the nine millimeter in his face and said, "Don't."

Somebody hit the lights.

It was the redheaded dorm assistant. Even drunk, he didn't like the looks of this.

Neither did I: the guy in front of me was not Jerome Lapps, but a slender, towheaded fellow in his midtwenties. The empty sleeve of his left arm was tucked into a sport-coat pocket.

I was a hell of a tough character: I'd just bested a cripple. Of course, I had to pull a gun to do it.

"What the hell ..." the redheaded kid began. His eyes were wide at the sight of the gun in my hand. The one-armed guy in front of me seemed less impressed.

"Police officer," I said to the redhead. "Go away."

He swallowed, nodded, and went.

"You're Jerome's roommate?" I asked the one-armed fellow.

"Yeah. Name's Robinson. Who are you? You really a cop?"

"I run a private agency," I said. "What branch were you in?"

"Army."

I nodded. "Marines," I said. I put the gun away. "You got a smoke?"

He nodded; with the one hand he had left, he got some Chesterfields out of his sport-coat pocket. Shook one out for me, then another for himself. He put the Chesterfields back and got out a silver Zippo. He lit us both up. He was goddamn good with that hand.

"Thank God them bastards left me with my right," he grinned sheepishly.

He sat on his bed. I sat across from him on Lapps'.

We smoked for a while. I thought about a punk kid cutting out pinups of Hitler while sharing a room with a guy who lost an arm over there. I was so happy I'd fought for the little fucker's freedoms.

"You're looking for Jerry, aren't you?" he asked. His eyes were light blue and sadder than a Joan Crawford picture.

"Yeah."

He shook his head. "Figured that kid would get himself into trouble."

"You roomed with him long?"

"Just for summer session. He's not a bad kid. Easy to get along with. Quiet."

"You know what he's got under his bed?"

"No."

"Suitcases full of stolen shit. If you need a new wristwatch, you picked the right roomie."

"I didn't know he was doing anything like that."

"Then what made you think he was going to get himself in trouble?"

"That black leather jacket of his."

"Huh?"

He shrugged. "When he'd get dressed up like a juvie. That black leather jacket. Dungarees. White T-shirt. Smoking cigarettes." He sucked on his own cigarette, shook his head. "He'd put that black leather jacket on, not every night, more like every once in a while. I'd ask him where he was going. You know what he'd say?"

"No."

"On the prowl."

I thought about that.

"Is his black leather jacket hanging in that closet you were lookin' in?"

"No," I said.

"Then guess where he is right now."

"On the prowl," I said.

He nodded.

12

Now I was on the prowl.

I went up Lakeshore, turned onto Sheridan, and followed it up to the Loyola El stop. The notepad on Lapps' desk had sent me here, to Rogers Park, the northernmost neighborhood in Chicago; beyond was Evanston. Here, in a three-block-wide and fourteen-block-long band between the lake and the El tracks was the middle-class residential area that would suit the kid's MO.

Lapps seemed partial to a certain type of building; according to Drury, many of the boy's burglaries were pulled off in tall, narrow apartment buildings consisting of small studio apartments. Same was true of where the two women who'd been killed had lived, and Katherine Reynolds, too.

First I would look for the dark-haired, black-leather-jacketed Lapps around the El stops—he had no car—and then I would cruise the side streets off Sheridan, looking in particular for that one type of building.

Windows rolled down, half-leaned out, I crawled slowly along, cutting the Plymouth's headlights as I cruised the residential neighborhoods; that way I didn't announce myself, and I seemed to be able to eyeball the sidewalks and buildings better that way. Now and then another car blinked its brights at me, but I ignored them and cruised on through the unseasonably cool July night.

About two blocks down from the Morse Avenue business district, on a street of modest apartment buildings, I spotted two guys running back the direction I'd come. The one in the lead was a heavyset guy in his T-shirt; close on his heels was a fellow in a plaid shirt. At first I thought one was chasing the other, but then it was clear they were together, and very upset.

The heavyset guy was slowing down and gesturing with open hands. "Where d'he go? Where d'he go?"

The other guy caught up to him and they both slowed down; in the meantime, I pulled over and trotted over to them.

"The cops, already!" the heavyset guy said joyously. He was a bald guy in his forties; five o'clock shadow smudged his face.

I didn't correct their assumption that I was a cop. I merely asked, "What gives, gents?"

The guy in the plaid shirt, thin, in his thirties, glasses, curly hair, pointed at nothing in particular and said, in a rush, "We had a prowler in the building. He was in my neighbor's flat!"

"I'm the janitor," the fat guy said, breathing hard, hands on his sides, winded. "I caught up to the guy in the lobby, but he pulled a gun on me." He shook his head. "Hell, I got a wife in the hospital, and three kids, that all need me unventilated. I let 'im pass."

"But Bud went and got reinforcements," the thin guy said, taking over, pointing to himself, "and my wife called the cops. And we took chase."

That last phrase almost made me smile, but I said, "Was it a dark-haired kid in a black leather jacket?"

They both blinked and nodded, properly amazed.

"He's going to hop the El," I said. I pointed to the thin guy. "You take the Morse El stop, I'll ..."

A scream interrupted me.

We turned toward the scream and it became a voice, a woman's voice, yelling, "He's up *there!*"

We saw her then, glimpsed between two rather squat apartment houses: a stout, older woman, lifting her skirts almost daintily as she barreled down the alley. I ran back there; the two guys were trailing well behind, and not eagerly. A lame horse could have gained the same lead.

The fleeing woman saw me, and we passed each other, her going in one direction, me in the other. She looked back and pointed, without missing a step, saying, "Up on the second-floor porch!" Then she continued on with her escape. It would have been a comic moment, if the alley hadn't been so dark and I hadn't been both running and scrambling for my nine millimeter.

I slowed to face the backyard of a two-story brick building and its exposed wooden back stairways and porches. Despite what the fleeing woman had said, the second-floor porch seemed empty, though it was hard to tell: it was dark back here, the El tracks looming behind me, casting their shadow. Maybe she meant the next building down....

As I was contemplating that, a figure rose on the second-floor porch and pointed a small revolver at me and I could see the hand moving, he was pulling the trigger, but his gun wasn't firing, wasn't working.

Mine was. I squeezed off three quick rounds and the latticework wood near him got chewed up, splinters flying. I didn't know if I'd hit him or not, and didn't wait to see; I moved for those steps, and bolted up one flight, and was at the bottom of the second when the figure loomed up above me, at the top of the stairs, and I saw him, his pale handsome face under long black greasy hair, his black leather jacket, his dungarees, and he threw the revolver at me like a baseball, and I ducked to one side, and swung my nine millimeter up just as he leaped.

He knocked me back before I could fire, back through the railing of the first-floor porch, snapping it into pieces like so many matchsticks, and we landed in a tangle on the grass, my gun getting lost on the trip. Then he was on top of me, like he was fucking me, and he was a big kid, powerful, pushing me down, pinning me like a wrestler, his teeth clenched, his eyes wide and maniacal.

I heaved with all my strength and weight and pitched him off to one side, but he didn't lose his grip on me, and we rolled, and I was on top now, only he hadn't given up, he hadn't let go, he had me more than I had him and that crazed, glazed look on his face scared the shit out of me. I couldn't punch him, even though I seemed to have the advantage, couldn't get my arms free, and he rocked up, as if he wanted to take a bite out of my face.

I was holding him down, but it was a standoff at best.

Then I sensed somebody coming up—that janitor and his skinny pal, maybe.

But the voice I heard didn't belong to either of them: "Is that the prowler?"

Still gripping my powerful captive by his arms, I glanced up and saw hovering over us a burly guy in swimming trunks holding a clay flowerpot in his hands.

"That's him," I said, struggling.

"That's all I wanted to know," the burly guy said, and smashed the flowerpot over the kid's head.

13

On the third smack, the flowerpot—which was empty—shattered into fragments and the kid's eyes rolled back and went round and white and blank like Orphan Annie's, and then he shut them. Blood was streaming down the kid's pale face. He was ruggedly handsome, even if Cornell Wilde was stretching it.

I got off him and gulped for my breath and the guy in his bathing trunks said, "Neighbors said a cop was after a prowler."

I stuck my hand out. "Thanks, buddy. I didn't figure the cavalry would show up in swim trunks, but I'll take what I can get."

His grasp was firm. He was an affable-looking, open-faced, hairy-chested fellow of maybe thirty-five. We stood over the unconscious kid like hunters who just bagged a moose.

"You a cop?"

"Private," I said. "My name's Nate Heller."

He grinned. "I thought you looked familiar. You're Bill Drury's pal, aren't you? I'm Chet Dickinson—I work traffic in the Loop."

"You're a cop? What's that, summer uniform?"

He snorted a laugh. "I live around here. My family and me was just walking back from a long day at the beach, when we run into this commotion. I sent Grace and the kids on home and figured I better check it out. Think we ought to get this little bastard to a hospital?"

I nodded. "Edgewater's close. Should we call for an ambulance? I got a car."

"You mind? The son of a bitch could have a concussion." He laughed again. "I saw you two strugglin', and I grabbed that flowerpot off a windowsill. Did the trick."

"Sure did."

"Fact, I mighta overdid it."

"Not from my point of view."

After Dickinson had found and collected the kid's revolver and contributed his beach towel to wrap the kid's head in, we drunk-walked Lapps to my car.

The burly bare-chested cop helped me settle the boy in the rider's seat. "I'll run over home, and call in, and get my buggy, and meet you over at Edgewater."

"Thanks. You know, I used to work traffic in the Loop."

"No kiddin'. Small world."

I had cuffs in the glove box; I cuffed the unconscious kid's hands behind him, in case he was faking it. I looked at the pleasant-faced cop. "Look—if anything comes of this, you got a piece of the reward action. It'll be just between us."

"Reward action?"

I put a hand on his hairy shoulder. "Chet—we just caught the goddamn Lipstick Killer."

His jaw dropped and I got in and pulled away, while he ran off, looking in those trunks of his like somebody in a half-assed track meet.

Then I pulled over around a corner and searched the kid. I figured there was no rush getting him to the hospital. If he died, he died.

He had two five-hundred-buck postal savings certificates in a pocket of his leather jacket. In his billfold, which had a University of Chicago student ID card in the name Jerome C. Lapps, was a folded-up letter, typed. It was dated last month. It said:

Jerry—

I haven't heard from you in a long time. Tough luck about the jail term. You'll know better next time.

I think they're catching up to me, so I got to entrust some of my belongings to you. I'll pick these suitcases up later. If you get short of cash, you can dip into the postal certificates.

I appreciate you taking these things off my hands when I was being followed. Could have dumped it, but I couldn't see losing all that jewelry. I'll give you a phone call before I come for the stuff.

George

I was no handwriting expert, but the handwritten signature sure looked like Lapps' own cramped handwriting from the inside cover of his calculus book.

The letter stuck me immediately as a lame attempt on the kid's part to blame the stolen goods stashed in his dorm room on some imaginary accomplice. Carrying it around with him, yet—an alibi in his billfold.

He was stirring.

He looked at me. Blinked. His lashes were long. "Who are you, mister? Where am I?"

I threw a sideways forearm into his stomach and doubled him over. He let the air out with a groan of pain that filled the car and made me smile.

"I'm somebody you tried to shoot, is who I am," I said. "And where you are is up shit creek without a paddle."

He shook his head, licked his lips. "I don't remember trying to shoot anybody. I'd never do a thing like that."

"Oh? You pointed a revolver at me, and when it wouldn't shoot, you hurled it at me. Then you jumped me. This just happened, Jerry."

A comma of greasy black hair fell to his forehead. "You ... you know my name? Oh. Sure." He noticed his open billfold on the seat next to us.

"I knew you before I saw your ID, Jerry. I been on your trail all day."

"I thought you cops worked in pairs."

"I don't work for the city. Right now, I'm working for the Robert Keenan family."

He recognized the name—anybody in Chicago would have—but his reaction was one of confusion, not alarm, or guilt, or anything else I might have expected.

"What does that have to do with me, mister?"

"You kidnapped their little girl, Jerry—you strangled her and then you tried to fuck her and then you cut her in pieces and threw the pieces in the sewer."

"What ... what are you ..."

I sidearmed him in the stomach again. I wanted to shove his head against the dash, but after those blows to the skull with that flowerpot, it might kill him. I wasn't particularly interested in having him die in my car. Get blood all over my new Plymouth. Peg would have a fit.

"You're the Lipstick Killer, Jerry. And I caught you going up the back stairs, like the cheap little sneak thief you are."

He looked down at his lap, guiltily. "I didn't kill those women."

"Really. Who did?"

"George."

The letter. The alibi.

"George," I said.

"Yeah," he said. "George did it."

"George did it."

"Sometimes I went along. Sometimes I helped him prepare. But I never did it. George did."

"Is that how you're going to play it?"

"George did it, mister. George hurt those women."

"Did George jack off the floor, or did you, Jerry?"

Now he started to cry.

"I did that," he admitted. "But George did the killings."

"JoAnn Keenan too?"

Lapps shook his head; his face glistened with tears. "He must have. He must have."

14

Cops in uniform, and plainclothes too, were waiting at the hospital when I deposited Lapps at the emergency room. I didn't talk to the kid after that, though I stuck around, at the request of a detective from Rogers Park.

The word spread fast. Dickinson, when he called it in, had spilled the Lipstick Killer connection. The brass started streaming in, and Chief of Detectives Storm took me off to one side and complimented me on my fine work. We decided that my visit to Lapps' dorm room would be off the record for now; in the meantime, South Side detectives were already on the scene making the same discoveries I had, only with the proper warrants.

I got a kick out of being treated like somebody special by the Chicago police department. Storm and even Tubbo Gilbert were all smiles and arms around my shoulder, when the press showed, which they quickly did. For years I'd been an "ex-cop" who left the force under a cloud in the Cermak administration; now, I was a "distinguished former member of the Detective Bureau who at one time was the youngest plainclothes officer on the force."

It soon became a problem, having the emergency area clogged with police personnel, politicians, and reporters. Lapps was moved upstairs, and everybody else moved to the lobby.

Dickinson, when he'd gone home, had taken time to get out of his trunks and into uniform, which was smart; the flashbulbs were popping around the husky, amiable patrolman. We posed for a few together, and he whispered to me, "We done good."

"You and your flowerpot."

"You're a hell of cop, Heller. I don't care what anybody says."

That was heartwarming.

My persistent pal Davis of the *News* was among the first of the many reporters to arrive and he buttonholed me with an offer of a grand for an exclusive. Much as I hated to, I had to turn him down.

From his expression you'd think I'd poleaxed him. "Heller turning down a payoff? Why?"

"This is too big to give to one paper. I got to let the whole world love me this time around." Most of the reward money—which was up to forty grand, now—had been posted by the various newspapers (though the city council had anted up, too) and I didn't want to alienate anybody.

"It's gonna be months before you see any of that dough," Davis whined. "It's all contingent upon a conviction, you know."

"I know. I can wait. I'm a patient man. Besides, I got a feeling the A-1 isn't going to be hurting for business after this."

Davis smirked. "Feelin' pretty cocky aren't you? Pretty smug."

"That's right," I said, and brushed by him. I went to the pay phones and called home. It was almost ten, but Peg usually stayed up at least that late.

"Nate! Where have you been ... it's almost ..."

"I know. I got him."

"What?"

"I got him."

There was a long pause.

"I love you," she said.

That beat reward money all to hell.

"I love you, too," I said. "Both of you."

I was slipping out of the booth when Lt. Kruger shambled over. His mournful-hound puss was twisted up in a grin. He extended his hand and we shook vigorously.

He took my arm, spoke in my ear. "Did you take a look at the letter in Lapps' billfold?"

I nodded. "It's his spare tire of an alibi. He told me 'George' did the killings. Is he sticking to that story?"

Kruger nodded. "Only I don't think there is a George."

"Next you'll be spoiling Santa Claus and the Easter Bunny for me."

"I don't think that's what he's up to."

"Oh? What is he up to, lieutenant?"

"I think it's a Jekyll and Hyde routine."

"Oh. *He's* George, only he doesn't know it. Split personality. There's a post-war scam for you."

Kruger nodded. "Insanity plea."

"The papers will love that shit."

"They love the damnedest things." He grinned again. "Tonight they even love you."

Chief of Detective Storm came and found me, shortly after that, and said, "There's somebody who wants to talk to you."

He led me back behind the reception counter to a phone, and he smiled quietly as he handed me the receiver. He might have been presenting an award of valor.

"Nate?" the voice said.

"Bob?"

"Nate. God bless you, Nate. You found the monster. You found him."

"It's early yet, Bob. The real investigation has just started ..."

"I knew I did the right thing calling you. I knew it."

I could tell he was crying.

"Bob. You give Norma my love."

"Thank you, Nate. Thank you."

I didn't know what to say. So I just said, "Thanks, Bob. Good night."

I gave a few more press interviews, made an appointment with Storm to come to First District Station the next morning and give a formal statement, shook Kruger's hand again, and wandered out into the parking lot. Things were winding down. I slipped behind the wheel of Plymouth and was about to start the engine when I saw the face in my rearview mirror.

"Hello, Heller," the man said.

His face was all sharp angles and holes: cheekbones, pock-marks, sunken dead eyes, pointed jaw, dimpled chin. His suit was black and well tailored—like an undertaker with style. His arms were folded, casually, and he was wearing kid gloves. In the summer.

He was one of Sam Flood's old cronies, a renowned thief from the 42 gang in the Patch. Good with a knife. His last name was Morello.

"We need to talk," he said. "Drive a while."

His first name was George.

15

"Sam couldn't come himself," George said. "Sends his regards, and apologies."

We were on Sheridan, heading toward Evanston.

"I was going to call Sam when I got home," I said, watching him in the rearview mirror. His eyes were gray under bushy black brows; spooky fucking eyes.

"Then you did make it to the kid's pad, before the cops." George sighed; smiled. A smile on that slash of a craggy face was not a festive thing.

"Yeah."

"And you got what Sam wants?"

"I do."

"The photo?"

"Yes."

"That's swell. You're all right, Heller. You're all right. Pull over into the graveyard, will you?"

Calvary Cemetery was the sort of gothic graveyard where Bela Lugosi and Frankenstein's monster might go for a stroll. I pulled in under the huge limestone archway and, when George directed, pulled off the main path onto a side one, and slowed to a stop. I shut the engine off. The massive granite wall of the cemetery muffled the roar of traffic on Sheridan; the world of the living seemed suddenly very distant.

"What's this about, George?" At Statesville, they say, where he was doing a stretch for grand theft auto, George was the prison shiv artist; an iceman whose price was five cartons of smokes, for which an individual who was annoying you became deceased.

Tonight George's voice was pleasant; soothing. A Sicilian disc jockey. "Sam just wants his photo, that's all."

"What's the rush?"

"Heller—what's it to you?"

"I'd rather turn it over to Sam personally."

He unfolded his arms and revealed a silenced Luger in his gloved right hand. "Sam says you should give it to me."

"It's in the trunk of the car."

"The trunk?"

"I had the photo in my coat pocket, but when I realized cops were going to be crawling all over, I slipped it in an envelope in my trunk, with some other papers."

That was the truth. I did that at the hospital, before I took Lapp inside.

"Show me," George said.

We got out of the car. George made me put my hands up and, gun in his right hand, he calmly patted me down with his left. He found the nine millimeter under my arm, slipped it out, and tossed it gently through the open window of the Plymouth onto the driver's seat.

Calvary was a rich person's cemetery, with mausoleums and life-size statues of dear departed children and other weirdness, all casting their shadows in the moonlight. George kept the gun in hand, but he wasn't obnoxious about it. I stepped around back of the Plymouth, unlocked the trunk, and reached in. George took a step forward. I doubled him over with the tire iron, then whacked the gun out of his hand, and swung the iron sideways against his cheek as he began to rise up.

I picked up his Luger and put a knee on his chest and the nose of the silenced gun against his bloody cheekbone. I would have to kill him. There was little doubt of that. His gray eyes were narrowed and full of hate and chillingly absent of fear.

"Was killing me Sam's idea, or yours?"

"Who said anything about killing you?"

I forced the bulky silenced nose of the gun into his mouth. Time for the Chicago lie-detector test.

Fear came into his eyes, finally.

I removed the gun, slowly, not taking any teeth, and said, "Your idea or Sam's?"

"Mine."

"Why, George?"

"Fuck you, Heller."

I put the gun in his mouth again.

After I removed it, less gently this time, cutting the roof of his mouth, he said through bloody spittle, "You're a loose end. Nobody likes loose ends."

"What's it to you, George?"

He said nothing; he was shaking. Most of it was anger. Some of it was fear. An animal smell was coming up off him.

"I said, what's it to you, George? What was your role in it?"

His eyes got very wide; something akin to panic was in them.

And then I knew.

Don't ask me how, exactly, but I did.

"You killed her," I said. It was part question, part statement. "*You* killed Sam's girlfriend. For Sam?"

He thought about the question; I started to push the gun back in his mouth and he began to nod, lips kissing the barrel.

"It was an accident. Sam threw her over, and she was posing a problem."

I didn't ask whether that problem was blackmail or going to the press or cops or what. It didn't much matter.

"So he had you hit her?"

"It was a fuck-up. I was just suppose to put the fear of God in her and get that fucking picture."

I pressed the gun into his cheek; the one that wasn't bloody. "That kid—Lapps ... he was your accomplice?"

"No! I didn't know who the hell he was. If we knew who he was, we coulda got that photo a long time ago. Why the fuck you think *you* were hired?"

That made sense; but not much else did. "So what was the deal, George?"

His eyes tightened; his expression said: *You know how it is.* "I was slapping her around, trying to get her to tell me where that picture was. I'd already tossed the place, but just sorta half-ass. She was arrogant. Spitting at me. All of a sudden her throat got cut."

Accidents will happen. "How did that kid get the photo album, then?"

"I heard something at the window; I looked up and saw this dark shape there, out on the fire escape ... thought it was a cop or something."

The black leather jacket.

"I thought *fuck it* and cut out," he said. "The kid must've come in, stole some shit, found that photo album someplace I missed, and left with it and a bunch of other stuff."

But before that, he washed the victim's wounds and applied a few bandages.

"What about the second girl?" I demanded. "Margaret Johnson? And the Keenan child?"

"I had nothing to do with them crimes. You think I'm a fuckin' psycho?"

I thought that one best left unanswered.

"George," I said calmly, easing the gun away from his face, "you got any suggestions on how we can resolve our differences, here? Can you think of some way both of us can walk out of this graveyard tonight?"

He licked his lips. Smiled a ghastly, blood-flecked smile. "Let bygones be bygones. You don't tell anybody what you know—Sam included—and I just forget about you working me over. That's fair. That's workable."

I didn't see where he got the knife; I hadn't seen a hand slip into a pocket at all. He slashed through my sleeve, but didn't cut me. When I shot him in the head, his skull exploded, but almost none of him got on me. Just my gun hand. A limestone angel, however, got wreathed in blood and brains.

I lifted up off him and stood there panting for a while. The sounds of muted traffic reminded me there was a world to go back to. I checked his pockets, found some Camels, and lit one up; kept the pack. Then I wiped my prints off his gun, laid it near him, retrieved my tire iron, put it back in the trunk, which I closed up, and left him there with his peers.

16

The phone call came late morning, which was a good thing: I didn't even make it into the office till after ten.

"You were a busy fella yesterday, Heller," Sam Flood's voice said cordially.

"I get around, Sam."

"Papers are full of you. Real hero. There's other news, though, that hasn't made the papers yet."

"By the afternoon edition, it'll be there."

We each knew what the other was talking about: soon Giorgio (George) Morello would be just another of the hundreds of Chicago's unsolved gangland killings.

"Lost a friend of mine last night," Sam said.

"My condolences. But I don't think he was such a good friend. He loused up that job with the girl, and he tried to sell me a cemetery plot last night."

The possibility of a phone tap kept the conversation elliptical; but we were right on track with each other.

"In other words," Sam said, "you only did what you had to do."

"That's right."

"What about that item you were gonna try to obtain for me?"

"It's in the hands of the U.S. Postal Service right now. Sealed tight—marked personal. I sent it to you at your liquor store on the West Side."

"That was prompt. You just got hold of the thing last night, right?"

"Right. No time to make copies. I didn't *want* a copy, Sam. Your business is your business. Anything I can do to make your happy home stay that way is fine with me. I got a wife, too. I understand these things."

There was a long, long pause.

Then: "I'll put your check in the mail, Heller. Pleasure doin' business with you."

"Always glad to hear from a satisfied customer."

There was a briefer pause.

"You wouldn't want to go on a yearly retainer, would you, Heller?"

"No thanks, Sam. I do appreciate it. Like to stay on your good side."

"That's wise, Heller. Sorry you had that trouble last night. Wasn't my doing."

"I know, Sam."

"You done good work. You done me a favor, really. If I can pay you back, you know the number."

"Thanks, Sam. That check you mentioned is plenty, though."

"Hey, and nice going on that other thing. That sex-maniac guy. Showed the cops up. Congratulations, war hero."

The phone clicked dead.

I swallowed and sat there at my desk, trembling.

While I had no desire to work for Sam Flood ever again, I did truly want to stay on his good side. And I had made no mention of what I knew was a key factor in his wanting that photo back.

It had little, if anything, to do with keeping his wife from seeing him pictured with his former girlfriend: it was the table of Sam's friends, glimpsed behind Sam and the girl in the photo.

Top mobsters from Chicago, New York, Cleveland, and Detroit. Some of kind of informal underworld summit meeting had been inadvertently captured by a nightclub photographer. Proof of a nationwide alliance of organized crime families, perhaps in a major meeting to discuss post-war plans.

If Sam suspected that I knew the true significance of that photo, I might not live to see my kid come into the world.

And I really wanted to.

17

A little over a week later, I was having lunch at Binyon's with Ken Levine, the attorney who had brought Bob Keenan and me together. The restaurant was a businessman's bastion, wooden booths, spartan decor; my old office was around the corner, but for years I'd been only an occasional customer here. Now that business was good, and my suits were Brooks Brothers not Maxwell Street, I could afford to hobnob on a more regular basis with the brokers, lawyers, and other well-to-do thieves.

"You couldn't ask for better publicity," Ken said. He was a small handsome man with sharp dark eyes that didn't miss anything and a hairline that was a memory.

"I'm taking on two more operatives," I said, sipping my rum cocktail.

"That's great. Glad it's working out so well for you." He made a clicking sound in his cheek. "Of course, the Bar Association may have something to say about the way that Lapps kid has been mistreated by Chicago's finest."

"I could bust out crying at the thought," I said.

"Yeah, well they've questioned him under sodium pentathol, hooked his nuts up to electrodes, done all sorts of zany stuff. And then they leak these vague, inadmissible 'confessions' to the papers. These wild stories of 'George' doing the crimes."

Nobody had connected George Morello to the case. Except me, of course, and I wasn't talking.

"The kid faked a coma for days," I said, "and then claimed amnesia. They had to do something."

Ken smiled wryly. "Nate, they brought in a priest and read last rites over him, to try to trick him into a 'deathbed' confession. They didn't feed him any solid food for four days. They held him six days without charging him or letting him talk to a lawyer. They probably beat the shit out of him, too."

I shrugged, sipped my cocktail. It was my second.

"Only it may backfire on 'em," Ken said. "All this dual personality stuff has the makings of an insanity plea. He's got some weird sexual deviation—his burglaries were sexually based, you know."

"How do you mean?"

"He got some kind of thrill out of entering the window of a strange apartment. He'd have a sexual emission shortly after entering. Must've been symbolic in his mind—entering through the window for him was like ... you know." He shrugged. "Apparently the kid's never had normal sex."

"Thank you, Dr. Freud."

Ken grinned. "Hey, I could get that little bastard off."

I was glad it wasn't Ken's case.

"Whatever his sex quirk," I said, "they tied him to the assault on that nurse, Katherine Reynolds. They matched his prints to one left in her apartment. And to a partial print on the Keenan kidnap note."

"The key word is partial," Ken said, raising a finger. "They got six points of similarity on the note. Eleven are required for a positive ID."

"They've got an *eyewitness* ID."

Ken laughed; there was genuine mirth in it. Lawyers can find the humor in both abstract thinking and human suffering.

"Their eyewitness is that old German janitor who was their best suspect till you nabbed Lapps. The old boy looked at four overweight, middle-aged cops and one seventeen-year-old in a lineup and somehow managed to pick out the seventeen-year-old. Before that, his description of the guy he saw was limited to 'a man in a brown raincoat with a shopping bag.' Did you know that that janitor used to be a butcher?"

"There was something in the papers about it. That doesn't mean he cuts up little girls."

"No. But if he lost his job during the war, 'cause of OPA restrictions, he could bear Bob Keenan a grudge."

"Bob wasn't with the OPA long enough for that to be possible. He was with the New York office. Jesus, Ken, what's your point, here?"

Like most attorneys, Ken was argumentative for the sheer hell of it; but he saw this was getting under my skin and backed off. "Just making conversation, Nate. That kid's guilty. The prosecutors are just goddamn lucky they got a mean little JD who carried Nietzche around and collected Nazi memorabilia. 'Cause without public opinion, they couldn't win this one."

Ken headed back to court and I sat working at my cocktail, wondering if I could get away with a third.

I shared some of Ken's misgivings about the way the Lapps case was being handled. A handwriting expert had linked the lipstick message on the late Margaret Johnson's wall with that of the Keenan kidnap note; then matched those to re-creations of both Lapps was made to give.

This handwriting expert's claim to fame was the Lindbergh case—having been there, I knew the Lindbergh handwriting evidence was a crock—and both the lipstick message and kidnap notes were printed, which made handwriting comparison close to worthless.

Of course, Lapps had misspelled some of the same words as in the note: "waite" and "safty." Only I'd learned in passing from Lt. Kruger that Lapps had been told to copy the notes, mistakes and all.

A fellow named Bruno Hauptmann had dutifully done the same in his handwriting samples, some years before. The lineup trick Ken had mentioned had been used to hand Hauptmann on a platter to a weak, elderly eyewitness, too. And the press had played their role in Bruno's railroading—one overeager reporter had written an incriminating phone number inside Hauptmann's apartment, to buy a headline that day, and that little piece of creative writing on wainscoting became an irrefutable key prosecution exhibit.

But so what? Bruno was (a) innocent and (b) long dead. This kid was alive, well, and psycho—and as guilty as the Nazi creeps he idolized. Besides which, what Ken had said about the kid's sexual deviation had made something suddenly clear to me.

I knew Lapps was into burglary for kicks, but I figured it was the violence against women that got him going. This business about strange buildings—and he'd had a certain of type of building, hadn't he, like some guys liked blondes or other guys were leg men—made a screwy sort of sense.

Lapps must have been out on the fire escape, peeking into Caroline Williams' apartment, casing it for a possible break-in, when he saw George slapping the girl around in the bedroom. He must have heard the Williams woman calling George by name—that planted the "George did it" seed—and got a new thrill when he witnessed George cut the woman's throat.

Then George had seen the dark, coplike figure out the window, got spooked, and lammed; and Lapps entered the apartment, spilled his seed, did his sick, guilty number washing and bandaging the corpse, and took various mementos, including undies and the photo album.

This new thrill had inspired Lapps to greater heights of madness, and the second girl—Margaret Johnson—had been all his. All his own twisted handiwork ... though perhaps in his mind George had done that, as well.

But Lapps, like so many men after even a normal sexual release, felt a sadness and even guilt and had left that lipstick plea on the wall.

That pretty nurse, Katherine Reynolds, had been lucky. Lapps hadn't been able to kill again; he'd stopped at assault—maybe he'd had his sexual release already, and his remorse kicked in before he could kill her. He'd even come back to help her.

What was bothering me, though, was the Keenan child. Nothing about Lapps' MO fit this crime. The building wasn't his "type." Kidnapping wasn't his crime, let alone dismembering a child. Had Lapps' thrill-seeking escalated into sheer depravity?

Even so, one thing was so wrong I couldn't invent any justification for it. Ken had said it: the kid had probably never had normal sex. The kid's idea of a fun date was going through a strange window and coming on the floor.

But rape had been attempted on the little girl. The coroner said so. Rape.

"Want some company, Heller?"

Hal Davis, with his oversize head and sideways smile, had already slid in across from me in the booth.

"Sure. What's new in the world of yellow journalism?"

"Slow day. Jeez, Heller, you look like shit."

"Thanks, Hal."

"You should be on top of the world. You're a local hero. A celebrity."

"Shut up, Hal."

Davis had brought a Scotch along with him. "Ain't this case a pip. Too bad they can't fry this kid, but in this enlightened day and age, he'll probably get a padded cell and three squares for the rest of his miserable life."

"I don't think they'll fry a seventeen-year-old, even in a case like this."

"What a case it's been. For you, especially."

"You got your share of mileage out of it, too, Hal."

He laughed; lit up a cigarette. Shook his head. "Funny."

"What is?"

"Who'd a thunk it?"

"Thunk what?"

He leaned over conspiratorially. His breath was evidence that this was not his first Scotch of the afternoon. "That the Keenan kidnapper really would turn out to be the Lipstick Killer. For real."

"Why not? He left his signature on Keenan's back fence. 'Stop me before I kill more ...'"

"That's the funny part." He snorted smugly. "Who do you think wrote that on the fence?"

I blinked. "What do you mean?"

Davis leaned across with a one-sided smirk that split his boyish face. "Don't be a jerk. Don't be so gullible. *I* wrote that there. It made for a hell of a byline."

I grabbed him by his lapels and dragged him across the table. His Scotch spilled and my drink went over and his cigarette went flying and his eyes were wide, as were those of the businessmen finishing up their two- and three-martini lunches.

"You *what*?" I asked him through my teeth.

"Nate! You're hurting me! Let go! You're makin' a scene ..."

I shoved him back against the booth. I got out. I was shaking. "You did do it, didn't you, you little cocksucker."

He was frightened, but he tried not to show it; he made a face, shrugged. "What's the big fucking deal?"

I grabbed him by the tie and he watched my fist while I decided whether to smash in his face.

Then the fist dissolved into fingers, but I retained my grip on his tie.

"Let's go talk to the cops," I said.

"I was just bullshitting," he said, lamely. "I didn't do it. Really. It was just the booze talking."

I put a hand around his throat and started to squeeze. His eyes popped. I was sneering at him when I said, "Stop me, Hal—before I kill more."

Then I shoved him against the wall, rattling some framed pictures, and got the hell out of there.

18

The cellar was lit by a single hanging bulb. There were laundry tubs and storage lockers, just like the basement where JoAnn Keenan was dismembered.

But this was not that basement. This was a slightly smaller one in a building near the "murder cellar," a tidy one with tools and cleaning implements neatly lining the walls, like well-behaved prisoners.

This was janitor Otto Bergstrum's domain.

"Why you want meet with me?" the thick-necked, white-haired Bergstrum asked.

Outside, it was rainy and dark. Close to midnight. I was in a drenched trenchcoat, getting Bergstrum's tidy cellar damp. I left my hat on and it was dripping, too.

"I told you on the phone," I said. "Business. A matter of money."

As before, the husky old fellow was in coveralls, his biceps tight against the rolled-up sleeves of his flannel shirt; his legs were planted well apart and firmly. His hands were fists and the fists were heavily veined.

"You come about reward money," he said. His eyes were blue and unblinking and cold under unruly salt-and-pepper eyebrows. "You try talk me out of claim my share."

"That's not it exactly. You see, there's going to be several people put in claims."

"Cops not eligible."

"Just city cops. I'm eligible."

"But they not."

"Right. But I have to kick back a few bucks to a couple of 'em, out of what I haul to shore."

"So, what? You think I should help you pay them?"

"No. I think you should kick your share back to me."

His eyes flared; he took a step forward. We were still a number of paces apart, though. Christ, his arms and shoulders were massive.

"Why should I do this?"

"Because I think you kidnapped the Keenan girl," I said.

He took a step back. His mouth dropped open. His eyes widened.

"I'm in clear," he said.

That was less than a denial, wasn't it?

"Otto," I said, "I checked up on you, this afternoon. Discreetly. You're a veteran, like me—only you served in the first war. On the other side."

He jutted his jaw. "I am proud to be German."

"But you were an American immigrant at the time. You'd been in this country since you were a kid. But still you went back home, to fight for the fatherland ... then after they lost their asses, you had the nerve to come back."

"I was not alone in doing such."

He wasn't, either: on the North Side, there was a whole organization of these German World War One vets who got together. They even had dinners with American vets.

"The Butcher's Union knew about you," I said, "but you were never a member."

"Communists," he said.

"You worked as a butcher in a shop on the West Side, for years—till meat shortages during the war ... this *last* war ... got you laid off. You were nonunion, couldn't find another butcher job ... with your background, anything defense-related was out. You wound up here. A janitor. It's your sister's building, isn't it?"

"You go to hell, mister."

"You know what I think, Otto? I think you blamed the New Deal for your bad deal. I think you got real mad at the government. I think you in particular blamed the OPA."

"Socialists," he said.

"Bob Keenan wasn't even in Chicago when you got laid off, you stupid old fart. But he was in the OPA now, and he was in the neighborhood. He had money, and he had a pretty little daughter. He was as good a place as any for Otto Bergstrum to get even."

"There is no proof of any of this. It is all air. Wind. You are the fart."

"What, did you get drunk, was it spur of the moment, or did you plan it? The kidnapping I can see. What I don't understand is killing the little girl. Did she start to make noise in bed, and you strangled her? Were you just too strong, and maybe drunk, and it was an accident of sorts?"

Now his face was an expressionless mask. His hands weren't fists any more. His eyes were hooded; his head was slack.

"What I really don't get, Otto, is the rape. Trying to rape a little girl. Was she already dead? You sick fucker."

He raised his head. "You have filthy mouth. Maybe I wash it out with lye."

"I'm going to give you a choice, old man. You can come with me, and come clean at Summerdale station. Or I can kill you right here."

"You have gun in your coat pocket?"

"I have gun in my coat pocket, yeah."

"Ah. But my friend has knife."

I hadn't heard him. I have no idea where he came from; coal bin, maybe. He was as quiet as nobody there. He was just suddenly behind me and he did have a knife, a long, sharp butcher knife that caught the single bulb's glow and reflected it, like the glint of a madman's eyes. Like the glint of this madman's eyes, as I stepped quickly to one side, the knife slashing down, cutting through the arm of my raincoat, cutting cloth and ripping a wound along my shoulder. My hand involuntarily released the gun, and even though both it and my hand were in the same coat pocket, I was fumbling for it, the gun caught in the cloth, my fingers searching for the grip....

I recognized this rail-thin, short-haired, sunken-cheeked young man as James Watson—but only from the papers. I'd never met him. He was the handyman at the nursery from which the kidnap ladder had been "stolen"; an Army vet and an accused child molester and, with Otto, a suspect in this case till I hauled Jerome Lapps onstage.

He was wearing a rain slicker, yellow, and one of those floppy yellow wide-brimmed rain hats; but he didn't look like he'd been outside. Maybe his raincoat was to keep the blood off.

He had the knife raised in such a corny fashion; raised in one fist, level with his head, and walking mummy-slow. His dark blue eyes were wide and his grin glazed and he looked silly, like a scarecrow with a knife, a caricature of a fiend. I could have laughed at how hokey this asshole looked, only Otto had grabbed me from behind as Watson advanced.

With my arms pulled back, one of them bleeding and burning from the slash of a knife that was even now red with my blood, I struggled but with little success. The old German janitor had me locked in his thick hands.

Watson stabbed savagely with the knife and I moved to the left and the blade, about half of it, went into Otto's neck and blood spurted. Otto went down, clutching his throat, his life oozing through his fingers, and I was free of him, and while Watson still had the knife in his hand—he'd withdrawn the blade almost as quickly as he'd accidentally sunk it into his cohort's throat—the handyman was stunned by the turn of events, his mouth hanging open, as if awaiting a dentist's drill. I grabbed his wrist with my two hands and swung his hand and his knife in a sudden arc down into his stomach.

The sound was like sticking your foot in thick mud.

He stood there, doing the oddest little dance, for several seconds, his hand gripped around the handle of the butcher knife, which I had driven in almost to the hilt. He looked down at himself with a look of infinite stupidity and danced some more.

I pushed his stupid face with the heel of my hand and he went ass-over-teakettle. He lay on his back twitching. He'd released the knife handle. I yanked the knife out of his stomach; there was a little hole in the rain slicker where the knife went in.

And the sound was like pulling your foot out of thick mud.

"You're the one who tried to rape that little girl, aren't you, Jim?"

He was blinking and twitching; a thin geyser of blood was coming from the hole in the yellow rain slicker.

"Poor old Otto just wanted to get even. Pull a little kidnap, make a little money off those socialist sons of bitches who cost him his job. But he picked a bad assistant in you, Jim. Had to play butcher on that dead little girl, trying to clean up after you."

There was still life in Watson's eyes. Otto was over near the laundry tubs, gurgling. Alive, barely.

I had the knife in one hand, and my blood was soaking my shirt under the raincoat, though I felt little if any pain. I gave some serious thought to waling away on Watson with the butcher knife; just carving the fucker up. But I couldn't quite cross the line.

I had George Morello's pack of Camels in my suit coat pocket. I dug them out and smoked while I watched both men die.

Better part of two cigarettes, it took.

Then I wiped off anything I'd touched, dropped the butcher knife near Watson, and left that charnel house behind; went out into a dark, warm summer night and a warm, cleansing summer rain, which put out the second cigarette.

It was down to the butt, anyway. I tossed it in a sewer.

19

The deaths of Otto Bergstrum and James Watson made a bizarre sidebar in the ongoing saga of the Lipstick Killer, but neither the cops nor the press allowed the "fatal falling out between friends" to influence the accepted scenario.

It turned out there was even something of a motive: Watson had loaned Otto five hundred dollars to pay off a gambling debt; Otto played the horses, it seemed. Speculation was that Watson, knowing Otto was due reward money from the Keenan case, had demanded payment. Both men were known to have bad tempers. Both had killed in the war—well, each in his individual war.

The cops never figured out how the two men had managed to kill each other with the one knife, not that anybody seemed to care. It was fine with me. Nobody had seen me in the vicinity that rainy night, or at least nobody who bothered to report it.

Lapps was indicted on multiple burglary, assault, and murder charges. His lawyers entered into what years later an investigative journalist would term "a strange, unprecedented cooperative relationship" with the State's Attorney's office.

In order to save their client from the electric chair, the defense lawyers—despite the prosecution's admission of the "small likelihood of a successful murder prosecution of Jerome Lapps"—advised the boy to cop a plea.

If Lapps were to confess to the murders of Caroline Williams, Margaret Johnson, and JoAnn Keenan, the State's

Attorney would seek concurrent life sentences. That meant parole in twenty years.

Lapps—reluctantly, I'm told—accepted the plea bargain, but when the boy was taken into a judge's presence to make a formal admission of guilt, he said instead, "I don't remember killing anybody."

The recantation cost him. Even though Lapps eventually gave everybody the confession they wanted, the deal was off: all he got out of it was avoiding the chair. His three life terms were concurrent with a recommendation of no parole. Ever.

He tried to hang himself in his cell, but it didn't take.

I took a ride on the Rock Island Rocket to Joliet to visit Lapps, about a year after he was sent up.

The visiting room at Stateville was a long narrow room cut in half by a long wide table with a glass divider. I'd already taken my seat with the other visitors when guards paraded in a handful of prisoners.

Lapps, like the others, wore blue denims and a blue-and-white striped shirt, which looked like a normal dress shirt, unless the wearer turned to reveal a stenciled number across the back. The husky, good-looking kid had changed little in appearance; maybe he was a little heavier. His dark, wavy hair, though no shorter, was cut differently—it was neater looking, a student's hair, not a JD's.

He sat and smiled shyly. "I remember you."

"You should. You tried to shoot me."

"That's what I understand. I'm sorry."

"You don't remember?"

"No."

"The gun you used was one you'd stolen. The owner identified it along with other stuff of his you took."

He shrugged; this was all news to him.

I continued: "The owner said the gun had been his father's and had been stuck in a drawer for seventeen years. Hadn't been fired for a long time."

His brow knit. "That's why the gun didn't go off, when I shot at you?"

"Yes. But a ballistics expert said the third shot *would* have gone off. You'd reactivated the trigger."

"I'm glad it didn't."

"Me too."

We looked at each other. My gaze was hard, unforgiving; his was evasive, shy.

"Why are you here, Mr. Heller?"

"I wanted to ask you a question. Why did you confess to all three murders?"

He shrugged again. "I had to. Otherwise, I'd be dead, my lawyers say. I just made things up. Told them what they wanted to hear. Repeated things back to them. Used what I read in the papers." One more shrug. Then his dark eyes tightened. "Why? You asked me like ... like you knew I didn't do them."

"You did one of them, Jerry. You killed Margaret Williams and you wrote that lipstick message on her wall."

Something flickered in his eyes. "I don't remember."

"Maybe not. But you also assaulted Katherine Reynolds, and you tried to shoot me. As far as I'm concerned, that's why you're here."

"You don't think I killed that little girl?"

"I know you didn't."

An eagerness sprang into his passive face. "Have you talked to my lawyers?"

I shook my head no.

"Would you talk to my ..."

"No. I'm not going to help you, Jerry."

"Why ... why are you telling this, then ...?"

My voice was barely above a whisper; this was just between us guys. "In case you're not faking. In case you really don't remember what you did. I think you got a right to know what you're doing time for. What you're really doing time for. And you did kill the second girl. And you almost killed the nurse. And you damn near killed me. That's why you're here, Jerry. That's why I'm leaving you here to rot, and don't bother repeating what I'm telling you, because I can out-lie every con in Stateville. I used to be a Chicago cop."

He was reeling. "Who ... who killed the first girl? Who killed that Caroline Williams lady?"

"Jerry," I said, rising to go, "George did it."

20

Lapps, as of this writing, is still inside. That's why, after all these years, as I edge toward senility in my Coral Springs condo, in the company of my second wife, I have put all this down on paper. The Parole for Lapps Committee requested a formal deposition, but I preferred that this take the same form, more or less, as other memoirs I've scribbled in my dotage.

Jerry Lapps is an old man now—not as old as me, but old. A gray-haired, paunchy old boy. Not the greasy-haired JD who I was glad to see go to hell and Stateville. He's been in custody longer than any other inmate in the Illinois prison system. Long before courses were offered to prisoners, he was the first Illinois inmate to earn a college degree. He then helped and advised other convicts with organizing similar self-help correspondence-course programs. He taught himself electronics and became a pretty fair watercolor artist. Right now he's in Vienna Prison, a minimum-security facility with no fences and no barred windows. He's the assistant to the prison chaplain.

Over the years, the press and public servants and surviving relatives of the murder victims—including JoAnn's sister Jane—have fought Lapps' parole. He is portrayed as the first of a particular breed of American urban monster—precursor to Richard Speck, John Wayne Gacy, and Ted Bundy.

Bob Keenan died last year. His wife Norma died three years ago.

Sam Flood—a.k.a. Sam Giancana—was hit in his home back in '75, right before he was supposed to testify before a Senate committee about Outfit/CIA connections.

Of the major players, Lapps is the only one left alive. Lapps and me.

What the hell. I've had my fill of revenge.

Let the bastard loose.

If he's faking rehabilitation like he once faked amnesia, if he hurts anybody else, shit—I'll haul the nine millimeter out of mothballs and hobble after him myself.

21

My son was born just before midnight, on September 27, 1947. We named him Nathan Samuel Heller, Jr.

His mother—exhausted after twelve hours of labor, face slick with sweat, hair matted down—never looked more beautiful to me. And I never saw her look happier.

"He's so small," she said. "Why did he take so long making his entrance?"

"He's small but he's stubborn. Like his mother."

"He's got your nose. He's got your mouth. He's gorgeous. You want to hold him, Nate?"

"Sure."

I took the little bundle, and looked at the sweet small face and experienced, for the first and only time before or since, love at first sight.

"I'm Daddy," I told the groggy little fellow. He made saliva bubbles. I touched his tiny nose. Examined his tiny hand—the miniature palm, the perfect little fingers. How could something so miraculous happen in such an awful world?

I gave him back to his mother and she put him to her breast and he began to suckle. A few minutes on the planet, and he was getting tit already. Life wasn't going to get much better.

I sat there and watched them and waves of joy and sadness alternated over me. It was mostly joy, but I couldn't keep from thinking that a hopeful mother had once held a tiny child named JoAnn in her arms, minutes after delivery; that another mother had held little Jerry Lapps in her gentle grasp. And Caroline Williams and Margaret Johnson were once babes in their mother's arms. One presumes even Otto Bergstrum and James Watson and, Christ, George Morello were sweet infants in their sweet mothers' arms, once upon a time.

I promised myself that my son would have it better than me. He wouldn't have to have it so goddamn rough; the depression was ancient history, and the war to end all wars was over. He'd want for nothing. Food, clothing, shelter, education, they were his birthright.

That's what we'd fought for, all of us. To give our kids what we never had. To give them a better, safer place to live in. Life, liberty, and the pursuit of happiness.

For that one night, settled into a hard hospital chair, in the glow of my brand-new little family, I allowed myself to believe that that hope was not a vain one. That anything was possible in this glorious post-war world.

KISSES OF DEATH

1

You can almost see it on the cover of *Photoplay* or *Modern Screen*, can't you, circa 1954? "I Was Marilyn Monroe's Bodyguard!" with a subhead reading, "A Private Eye's Hollywood Dream Assignment!" ... but in the end, "A New York Nightmare of Depravity" was more like it, worthy of *Confidential* or *Whisper*.

Not that Miss Monroe was involved in any of that depravity—no such luck—though we did have a promising first meeting, and it was in neither Hollywood nor New York, but in my native Chicago, at the Palmer House, where the A-1 Detective Agency was providing security for the American Booksellers Association's annual convention.

I didn't do any of the security work at the booksellers shindig myself—that was for my staff, and a few add-on ops I rounded up. After all, I was Nathan Heller, president of the A-1, and such lowly babysitting was simply beneath my executive position.

Unless, of course, the baby I was sitting was Miss Marilyn Monroe, curled up opposite me on a couch, sweetly sitting in her suite's sitting room, afternoon sunlight coming in behind her, making a hazy halo of her carefully coifed platinum pageboy.

"I hope this isn't a problem for you," she said, shyly, with only a hint of the mannered, sexy exaggeration I'd noted on the screen. "Such short notice, I mean."

Normally I didn't cancel a Friday night date with a Chez Paree chorus girl to take on a bodyguard job, but I only said, "I had nothing planned. My pleasure, Miss Monroe."

"Marilyn," she corrected gently. "Is it Nate, or Nathan?"

Her manner was surprisingly deferential, and disarmingly reserved. Like other movie stars I'd encountered over the years, from George Raft to Mae West, she was smaller than I expected, though her figure lived up to expectations, partly because her black short-sleeved cotton sweater and her dark gray Capri pants were strategically snug.

"Nate's fine," I said. "Or Nathan."

I would gladly have answered to Clem or Philbert, if she were so inclined. I was forty-seven years of age, and she was, what? Twenty-five? Twenty-six? And I felt like a schoolboy, tongue thick, hands awkward, penis twitching, rearing its head threateningly as I crossed my legs.

Her barefoot casualness (her toenails, like her fingernails, were painted a platinum that matched her hair) was offset by the flawlessness of her surprisingly understated makeup, her complexion luminously, palely perfect, a glorious collaboration between God and Max Factor. The startling red of her lipsticked lips was ideal for her world-famous smile—sex-saturated, open-mouthed, accompanied by a tilt-back of the head and bedroom-lidded eyes—only I never saw that smile once, that afternoon.

Instead, only rare tentative fleeting smiles touched those bruised baby lips, and for all her sex appeal, the in-person Marilyn Monroe's undeniable charisma invoked in me unexpected stirrings, which is to say, Not Entirely Sexual. I wanted to protect this girl. And she did seem a girl to me, for all her womanly charms.

"I read about you in *Life*," she said, dark blue eyes twinkling.

She'd read about *me* in *Life*. Was she kidding?

Actually, she probably wasn't. Last year the magazine had done a spread on me, and my career, touching on the Lindbergh kidnapping, the Sir Harry Oakes murder, and several other of my more headline-worthy cases of years past, but focusing more on the current success of my Hollywood branch of the A-1, which was developing into the movie stars' private detective agency of choice.

On the other hand, I'd read about her not only in *Life*, but *Look*, and the *Saturday Evening Post*, and *Esquire*, not to mention the *Police Gazette*, *Coronet*, and *Modern Man*. She was also the reason why I hadn't, in June of 1953, gotten around to taking down a certain 1952 calendar as yet. My most vivid memory of Miss Monroe, prior to meeting her face to face, was a rear view of her walking slowly away from the camera in a movie called *Niagara* (which I walked away from after her character got prematurely bumped off).

"When Ben told me about the party tonight, at Riccardo's," she said, "I simply had to be there. I'm afraid I invited myself ..."

As if there'd be an objection.

" ... and Ben suggested we ask you to accompany us. He thinks it's a necessary precaution."

"I agree with him," I said. "That joint'll be crawling with reporters."

She shivered. "Oh, and I've had my fill of the press today, already."

Marilyn Monroe was in town on a press swing to promote the imminent release of *Gentlemen Prefer Blondes*; when I'd arrived at her suite, she had just wrapped up an interview with Irv Kupcinet, of the *Sun Times*.

"If they see me at your side," I said, "they may be more inclined to behave themselves."

"That's sort of what Ben said. He said people know you in Chicago. That you have quite a reputation."

"Reputations can deceiving."

"Oh yes," she said with a lift of her eyes and a flutter of lashes. "Nathan, can I get you something to drink?"

"A Coke would be nice."

She flashed just a hint of the famous smile, said, "I'll have one, too," rose and walked to a little bar in one corner, and in those painted-on Capri pants, she provided a rear view even more memorable than *Niagara*.

Soon she was behind the bar, pouring Coca-Cola over ice, saying, "How did you meet Ben? I met him on monkey business."

"Met him how?"

She walked over to where I was sitting, a tumbler in either hand, a study in sexy symmetry as her breasts did a gentle braless dance under the sweater. "On the movie—*Monkey Business*. Ben wrote it. That was a good role for me. Nice and funny, and light. How did *you* meet him?"

I took my Coke from her. "You better let Ben tell it."

I figured that was wise, because I had no idea where or when I'd first met Ben Hecht, though according to Ben we'd known each other since I was a kid. I had no memory of encountering Hecht back in those waning days of the so-called Chicago literary Renaissance of the late teens and early twenties, though when he approached me to do a Hollywood job for him, a few years ago, he insisted we were old friends ... and since he'd been the client, who was I to argue?

Hecht, after all, was a storyteller, and reinventing his own life, revising his own memories into better tales, was in his nature.

She sat up, now, and forward, hands folded in her lap around the glass of Coke, an attentive schoolgirl. "Ben says your father had a radical bookshop."

"That's right," I said. "We were on the West Side, and most of the literary and political shenanigans were centered in Tower Town ..."

"Tower Town?"

"That's the area that used to be Chicago's Greenwich Village; still is, sort of, but it's dying out. On the Near North Side. But most of the freethinkers and radicals and artsy types found their way into Heller's Books, from Clarence Darrow to Carl Sandburg."

Her eyes went wide as Betty Boop's. "You know Carl Sandburg?"

"Sure. He used to play his guitar and sing his god-awful folks songs in this little performance area we had."

Her sigh could only be described as wistful. "I love his poetry."

"Yeah, he's become a big deal, hasn't he? Nice guy."

Hope danced in the wide eyes. "Will he be there tonight?"

Imagine a homely wart like Charlie getting a dish like this warmed up over him.

"I kind of doubt it. He doesn't get back to Chicago all that much."

Her disappointment was obvious, but she perked herself up, saying, "Ben's arranged this party as a benefit for Maxwell Bodenheim, you know."

"Are you serious?"

Misinterpreting my displeasure as something positive, she nodded and said, "Oh, yes. Ben said Mr. Bodenheim and his wife flew in from New York last night. Do you know him?"

"Yeah. Yeah, I know Max. I'm surprised you've even heard of him, Marilyn."

"I read a lot of poetry," she said. "His *Selected Poems* is a delightful collection."

Who was I to rain on her parade? How could she know that Bodenheim, who I vividly remembered from childhood, had been a womanizing, sarcastic, self-important, drunken leach? The only writer my softhearted father had ever banished from his store, when he caught Bodenheim shoplifting copies of his own books.

"I haven't thought of that guy in probably thirty years," I said. "I didn't even know he was still alive."

Her brow furrowed with sympathy. "Ben says Mr. Bodenheim has fallen on hard times. It's difficult to make a living as a poet."

I sipped my Coke. "He used to write novels, too. He had some bestsellers in the twenties."

Sexy potboilers, with titles like *Replenishing Jessica*, *Georgie May*, and *Naked on Roller Skates*, that had seemed pretty racy in their day; *Jessica* had even been busted as pornography. Of course, in the modern era of Erskine Caldwell and Mickey Spillane, the naughty doings of Bodenheim's promiscuous jazz-age heroines would probably seem pretty mild.

Still, if Bodenheim was broke, it was only after squandering the fortune or two a bestselling writer would naturally accrue.

"I just think it's wonderful of Ben to help his old friend out like this," she said, her smile radiant, as madonnalike as she imaged Hecht's intentions to be saintly.

Bodenheim was indeed an "old friend" of Hecht's, but my understanding was that they'd had a major falling out, long ago; in fact, while I don't remember ever meeting Hecht in the old days, I do remember my father talking about how violently these two one-time literary collaborators had fallen out. Hecht had even written a novel, *Count Bruga*, lampooning his pretentious former crony, to which Bodenheim replied with his own novel, *Duke Herring*, about a self-centered sellout clearly patterned on Hecht.

The gathering tonight at Riccardo's was a Renaissance reunion, organized by Hecht, who was one of that movement's stellar graduates, albeit not in the literary way of such figures as Sandburg, Vachel Lindsay, Sherwood Anderson, Edgar Lee Masters, and Margaret Anderson. Hecht—whose archly literary novels and would-be avant-garde pornography of the twenties had made him a king among local bohemians—had literally gone Hollywood.

After the success of his play *The Front Page*, a collaboration with Charlie MacArthur, another former Chicago newspaperman, Hecht began a wildly successful screenwriting career—*Scarface, Gunga Din, Spellbound,* and *Notorious,* to name a few of his credits—that would be impressive by anybody's standards. Except, perhaps, those of the literary types among whom he'd once dwelled.

Like Bodenheim.

Of course, I didn't figure—other than Bodenheim—there would be many people at the party that Hecht would owe any apology to. The crowd that Ben and Bodenheim had hung out with, sharing the pages of literary magazines, and the stages of little theaters and the wild and wooly Dill Pickle Club, was pretty well thinned out by now. The most exotic demise was probably that of Harriet Monroe (presumably no relation to Marilyn); the editor of the prestigious magazine *Poetry*, Harriet had died in 1936, on some sort of mountain-climbing expedition in Peru (Sherwood Anderson also died in South America, but less exotically, succumbing to peritonitis on a goodwill tour). Vachel Lindsay had died a suicide, Edgar Lee Masters died broke in a convalescent home. This poetry was a rough racket.

The beautiful, enigmatic (i.e., lesbian) editor of the *Little Review*, Margaret Anderson, wasn't dead, but she might as well have been: she lived in Paris. I figured the party attendees would mostly be Renaissance refugees who had drifted back into the newspaper business, from whence most of the players had come in the first place, seasoned veterans of Schlogl's, the legendary Loop tavern where *Daily News* reporters gathered, even those without literary pretensions.

Of course, Riccardo's was a newspaper hangout in general, and the entertainment scribes Marilyn had already encountered this trip—Kup, Herb Lyon, Anna Nangle, among others—might be there, as well. I knew all of them and could keep them at bay in a friendly way.

I sipped my Coke. "I gather you and Ben are embarking on some sort of project together."

"Well, we're seriously discussing—"

And a knock at the door interrupted her. I offered to answer it for her, and did, and as if he'd arrived specifically to answer my question, there was Ben.

"Madhouse down there," he said, gesturing with a thumb, as if pointing to Hell, but in reality only meaning the floor where the meetings and seminars of the ABA were being held.

Ben Hecht, a vigorous sixty years of age, brushed by me and went over to greet Marilyn, who rose from the couch to give him a Hollywood hug. His frame was square, large-boned, just under six foot, his attire rather casual for a business occasion, a brown sport jacket over a green sport shirt; a Russian Jew, he looked more Russian than Jewish—a pleasant, even handsome-looking man with an oval head, salt-and-pepper curly hair, a high forehead that was obviously in the process of getting higher, trimmed mustache, deep-blue slightly sunken eyes, and strong jaw worthy of a leading man.

She sat back down, and he nestled next to her, and took her hands in his as if about to propose marriage.

"I talked to the Doubleday people," Ben said, "and they're very excited."

Her eyes Betty-Booped again. "Really?"

"They did somersaults over the idea."

Now she winced. "I still think I'm a little young to be writing my life story ..."

"You're the hottest thing in show business, kid. Strike while the iron is hot. You liked the sample chapters I wrote, didn't you?"

"I *loved* them." She turned to me, and I was relieved to see that one of them realized I was still there. "We spent an afternoon at the Beverly Hills Hotel, Ben and I, with me talking into a tape recorder, and then a few days later we met again. Ben had turned my ramblings into something marvelous. I laughed ... I cried ..."

"Well," he said, withdrawing a cigar from a silver case from inside his sport jacket, "you'll laugh and cry with joy when you hear the deal Doubleday's offering. Plus, I talked to some people from the *Ladies' Home Journal*, and they're going to make an offer to serialize."

For a guy famous for writing ping-pong back-and-forth dialogue, Ben nonetheless spoke in paragraphs, though the words did flow at a machine-gun clip.

"Oh, Ben ... this is so wonderful ..."

He bit off the end of his cigar. "Kid, they're going to pay you bushel baskets of money, and the end result is, publicity for you. Only in America."

"Ben, how can I ever repay you?"

It was a question millions of American men would have died to hear Marilyn Monroe ask.

Ben, patting his jacket pockets as if he were frisking himself, replied with, "You got a light?"

She nodded and pranced over to the bar and got some hotel matches and came bouncing back and fired up his Cuban. It had a strong, pleasant aroma, but the mixture of it and Marilyn's Chanel Number Five was making me a little queasy.

I asked, "What time's the party?"

"They got a buffet over there for us," Ben said, "at seven. I'm kind of the host, so I'll head over a little early. Marilyn, what time would you like to make your appearance?"

"Maybe around eight," she offered. Then she looked at me. "Could you meet me in the lobby, Nathan, and escort me over?"

"Be delighted."

She stood. "Then you boys better scoot. I have to get ready."

"You are ready," Ben said, but he was rising at her command just the same. He gestured with his cigar in hand. "These are writers and poets, kid. Come as you are."

"I'll wear something nice and casual," she promised. "But I'd like to relax with a nice long hot bubble bath ..."

That was a pretty image to leave on, so we did. In the hall, as we waited for the elevator, I said, "*Boden*heim?"

"Yeah," Hecht said, as if throwing a benefit for his arch literary enemy was a natural thing to do. "We flew him and his wife in. I got them over at the Bismarck, if he hasn't burned it down by now."

"What's he need a benefit for?"

Hecht snorted, spoke around his cigar. "Are you kidding? He's been living in Greenwich Village for the last, I don't know, twenty years. Poor bastard's turned into a bum. Complete alky. You know how he makes his living, such as it is? Hawking his poems on street corners, pinnin' 'em on a fence, sellin' 'em for quarters and dimes."

"Jesus. Even I wouldn't wish that on him. I mean, he was famous ... respected...."

"There was a time," Hecht said, and the sunken eyes grew distant, "when he was near the peak of poetry in this nation. Ezra Pound wrote him goddamn fan letters. William Carlos Williams, Conrad Aiken, Marianne Moore, all expressed their public admiration. Now? Now the son of bitch is sleeping on park benches and, when he's lucky, in flophouses."

"What's this about a wife?"

Hecht got a funny smile going; he flicked ashes from the cigar in the wall ashtray by the elevator buttons. "Her name's Ruth. He looks like shit, but she's kind of foxy, in a low-rent kind of way." Hecht shook his head, laughed. "Son of a bitch always did have a way with the ladies. You know the stories, don't you, about the suicides?"

I did. There was a period in the twenties, shortly after Bodenheim traded Chicago for New York, that the national papers were filled with the stories of young women driven to suicide by the fickle attentions of the author of *Replenishing Jessica*.

"I know you fancy yourself a ladies' man, Nate," Hecht said with a sly grin. "But committing suicide over your favors never has become a national fad, now, has it?"

"Not yet," I granted, and the elevator finally arrived. We stepped on. Hecht pushed the button for his floor and I hit LOBBY. We had the elevator to ourselves, so our conversation remained frank.

"What's all this about you writing Marilyn's autobiography? Since when are you reduced to that kind of thing, or are you trying to get a piece of that sweet girl's personality?"

Hecht had his own reputation as a ladies' man, or at least, womanizer.

He shrugged. "Straight ghost job. Good payday. I don't always sign my work, kid. Hell, if I put my name on every script I doctored, I'd be the most famous asshole in Hollywood."

"Well, doesn't scriptwriting pay better than books?"

"Hell yes." His voice remained jaunty but his expression turned grave. "But, frankly, kid—I got my ass in a wringer with this big fat mouth of mine. I'm blacklisted in England, you know, and if a producer uses me on a script, he can't put my name on the British prints, and if the Brits find out my name was on the American version, they might pass on the thing, anyway." His sigh was massive. "If you ever hear me gettin' messed up in politics again, slap my face, okay?"

"What are friends for?"

Hecht, whose apolitical nature was probably the reason why my father's radical bookshop was an unlikely place for us to have met, had gotten uncharacteristically political, right after the war. Specifically, he got vocal about Israel, outspoken in his opinion that England was the enemy of that emerging state, publicly praising Irgun terrorists for blowing up British trains and robbing British banks and killing British "tommies."

"Maybe it's for the best," he said, as the bell rang and the door drew open at his floor. "It's putting me back in the world of books, where I belong. Hey, I talked to Simon and Schuster this afternoon, and they're makin' an offer on *my* autobiography.... See you at Riccardo's, kid!"

And with that final machine-gun burst of verbiage, he was gone.

2

Just to be safe, I returned to the Palmer House at seven thirty, walking over from my suite of offices at the Monadnock Building, going in on the State Street side, through the business arcade and up the escalator to the vast high-ceilinged lobby, a cathedral-like affair with arched balconies, Roman travertine walls, and an elaborately painted Italian classical ceiling depicting gods and goddesses, which was only fitting considering who I was escorting tonight.

And since Hollywood divinity occupies a time and space continuum all its own, I had plenty of opportunity, seated comfortably in one of the velvet-upholstered chairs, to study each and every shapely nude, and near-nude, cloud-perched goddess.

As my delight at this assignment gradually wore to irritation (shortly after nine), I began toying with calling up to Miss Monroe's suite to see if I'd misunderstood when I was to pick her up, or if she'd run into a problem, and just as irritation was bleeding into indignation (nine thirty), she stepped out of an elevator, a vision of twentieth-century womanhood that put to shame the classical dames floating above me.

She wore a simple black linen dress, spaghetti straps and a fairly low, straight-across-the-bosom neckline—no sign of a bra, or any pantyline, either; her heels were black strappy sandals, her legs bare. No jewelry, a small black purse in hand. Doffing my coconut-palm narrow-brim hat, I rose to approach her as she click-clacked toward me across the marble floor and by the time I'd slipped my arm in hers, and gazed into that radiant face with its blazingly red-lipsticked baby-doll pout, my annoyance disappeared, and delight had bloomed again.

She issued no apology for her tardiness, but what she said instead was much better: "Don't *you* look handsome."

And for the first time I witnessed, in person, the practiced, patented open-mouthed smile, as she stroked the sleeve of my green Dacron sport jacket, then straightened and smoothed the lighter-green linen tie that matched my sport shirt, under which my heart went pitty pat.

"I thought bodyguards tried to blend into the woodwork," she said, eyeing my canary-yellow lightweight slacks.

"This bodyguard wants to be noticed," I said, as we walked through a lobby whose patrons were wide-eyed with wonder at the presence among them of this goddess. "Not that anyone will ..."

In back of the cab, on our way to Riccardo's, I ventured a question: "Do you mind if I ask something a little personal?"

"Ask and see."

"Is what I read about in the papers true, about you and Joe DiMaggio?"

She shrugged. "We've been dating, kind of off and on."

"Is it 'on' right now?"

"Off."

"Ah," I said. "I'm sorry."

"Are you really, Nathan?"

"No."

She smiled at that. Then, looking out the window at the Loop gliding by, she said rather absently, "I'd never heard of him."

"Never heard of Joltin' Joe?"

She looked back and me and a tiny laugh bubbled in her throat. "It was a blind date. My girlfriend said he was a famous ballplayer who liked blondes. I didn't even know what kind of ballplayer she meant, football or baseball or what. Didn't want to look any dumber than I already did, but he was a real sweetheart on the date, and you should've seen people slapping him on the back, asking him for autographs. They were completely ignoring me."

"And you liked that?"

"I respected it.... Are you married, Nathan?"

"Not right now."

Riccardo's was a converted warehouse at 437 North Rush; it began in '34 as a hole-in-the-wall gathering place for artists, writers, and theatrical types, but had been revamped and expanded a decade ago to accommodate the wider clientele its arty atmosphere and exotic reputation attracted.

The evening was pleasantly warm, with just the right hint of lake breeze, and the tables that spilled out from under the awning onto the sidewalk were packed with patrons enjoying dinner and drinks and a magnificent view of the parking lot. Heads swiveled and eyes widened as I guided Marilyn through the tables and into the restaurant, which somehow managed an intimate ambience despite expansive, open seating and bright lighting designed to show off the framed paintings that were everywhere.

"Looks more like an art gallery than a restaurant," Marilyn said breathlessly, her gaze skimming above the heads of diners who were admiring the work of art walking among them.

"It's both," I said, moving her gently through the crowd. "This main dining room is an exhibit hall for young midwestern artists."

"What a lovely notion! So the paintings are constantly changing?"

I nodded. "One-man shows lasting a month."

This month's genius seemed adept at filling canvases with dull gray backgrounds on which danced amoebalike blobs of garish purple, red, and green.

"Ah," I said, "here's Ric ..."

In a black suit and tie, tall, slender, a youthful fifty with his gray crew cut and black eyebrows and mustache, looking like a Mephisthophelean maitre d', Ric Riccardo approached, eyes twinkling, hand outstretched.

"The Chicago Sherlock," he said, as we shook hands. "And no introduction is required of this lovely lady ..."

He gently took her fingertips in his and kissed the back of her hand and she smiled and raised her eyebrows, appreciation murmuring behind her kiss of a pursed smile.

"Marilyn, this is Ric Riccardo."

She frowned. "You don't look much like Desi Arnaz."

Ric looked mildly wounded. I wasn't sure whether she was kidding or not, but somehow with her it didn't matter.

"This is the original," I said, "and he's Italian, not Cuban."

Her bare shoulders lifted and sat themselves down, doing a fine job of it, too, I must say. "I just love the idea of your restaurant, Mr. Riccardo! You're a true patron of the arts."

Ric made a dismissive gesture. "I'm afraid I only did it to have a place to hang my own canvases."

"You're an artist, too?"

"I've never been able to decide whether I paint badly," Ric sighed, "or whether people just can't understand what I paint. But at least, here, I sell a canvas now and then."

"Don't let him kid you," I told her, "his artwork's even better than his veal scaloppine."

Ric's eyes narrowed. "Which brings us to a difficult subject—my friends, you've missed the buffet, and I'm afraid the party has moved from my private dining room into the bar."

He led us down into the lower level, where I spotted Ben chatting with a pair of *Trib* talents, obsessive Sherlock Holmes buff Vincent Starrett and literary section editor Fanny Butcher. Here and there were the likes of bookseller Stuart Brent, *Herald American* columnist Bob Casey, various other well-known local scribes, John Gunther, Bill Leonard, Bob Cromie, among the bigger names. Mostly, as I had predicted, the crowd consisted of second-stringers and tail-end members from the Renaissance movement, who had gone back to the newspaper world that spawned them.

"Oooo," Marilyn said, "look at that odd-shaped bar!"

"It's a big artist's palette," I said.

"Oh, it is!" And her laughter chimed.

"Our murals back behind there," Ric said proudly, as he led us to a corner table for two, plucking the "reserved" sign off, "are the work of our city's most well-known artists—the Albrights, Aaron Bohrod, Vincent D'Agostino ..."

"And Desi Arnaz, here," I said.

And our host smiled, bowed, and—with us deposited at our cozy table—moved on. Like Ben Hecht, Ric was a pragmatic Renaissance survivor, an artist turned businessman. And like Ben, Ric liked to think he was still a bohemian at heart.

For all its premeditated hipness, however, Ric's restaurant bore the square stigmata of Italian restaurants immemorial: instead of the cool tinklings of jazz piano, the air resounded with the strains of "O Sole Mio," accompanied by violin, mandolin, and concertina, courtesy of strolling singers and musicians in ruffled sleeves and satin trousers.

Wandering in from the dining room and sidewalk café, where they provided a welcome backdrop for couples romantically dining, came a trio of these singers with a violinist in tow, warbling "Come Back to Sorrento." This was a misguided sortie into enemy territory, as Ben and other self-styled intellectual and literary lights attending the reunion glanced at them irritably over cocktail glass rims and cigarettes-in-hand.

A slender ponytail brunette, her olive complexion a stark contrast next to her short-sleeved cream-color dress, planted herself in front of the musicians, hands pressed around a tall glass, swaying to their serenade. At first glance she seemed attractive, even strikingly so, and I pegged her for her midtwenties.

"She's having fun," Marilyn said, not at all judgmentally.

As the musicians moved through the bar, and closer to us, and the brunette danced sensuously along, I got a closer look at her. The dress was a frayed secondhand-store frock, and she had to be in her thirties. Her big brown eyes were cloudy and dark-circled, her wide mouth slack.

This girl wasn't tipsy: she was a lush.

About this time, the musicians noticed Marilyn—or at least noticed a beautiful blonde—and made their way to our table. I was digging for a half dollar to tip them, and make them go away, when the slender bombed brunette inserted herself between us and the strolling musicians and hip-swayed to their music in a manner that would suit Minksy's better than Riccardo's.

Marilyn's glance at me was more sad than disapproving.

The brunette clutched the arm of the nearest singer—a handsome if chubby kid in his twenties, the tenor—and her other hand began moving up and down the thigh of his satin pants.

"Gentlemen!" a male voice cried, above the syrupy strains. "Please cease."

And an absurd figure who might have walked in off a burlesque stage appeared at the fringe of this little tableau, positioning himself alongside the violinist, a foul-smelling corncob pipe in one hand, a double-shot glass of straight whiskey in the other. The four musicians trailed off into stunned silence, and their eyes traveled from the drunken dame to the latest character in this farce, stooped, obviously inebriated, a frail sack of bones swimming in a dark, shabby, slept-in suit set off ever so nattily by a dark frayed food-stained tie and shoes that had long since exploded in wear.

His face was misshapen from years of drink, the blobby careless first draft of an indifferent sculptor, skull beneath the flesh asserting itself as his features threatened to fall off, his complexion a mottled albino, eyes dark rheumy haunted pools, nose a lumpy sweet potato, mouth a thin crumpled line. His hair, unkempt and shaggy as it was, his ears half-covered, sideburns bordering on mutton chop, was the garish reddish brown of a Mercurochrome dye job; it might have been a wig, had this pitiful creature been able to afford one.

"Could it be," he said, revealing a jack-o'-lantern smile, his near-toothlessness giving him a Karloff lisp, "that angelic choristers of heaven have invaded this bistro, wings tipped with music vibrating like a flock of wild swans skimming the surface of some enchanted sea?"

"Shut up, Max," the brunette said; she had a husky voice that under the right circumstances might have been sexy.

"Who is that?" Marilyn whispered.

"The guest of honor," I said.

And this was indeed Maxwell Bodenheim, an astonishing husk of the tall, slim, golden-haired ladies' man I remembered from my father's bookshop; back then, only his eyebrows had been a devilish red-brown.

He leaned against the shoulder of the violinist. "And are these the heartwarming, bell-like tones of a Heifetz? Or does the angel Gabriel lurk in your barrel-like form?"

"Max!" she said. "Can't a girl *dance*?"

He raised the whiskey glass sloshingly, a parody of a toast, underlined by the threat of flinging it in the nearest face (not much of one, because Bodenheim was unlikely to waste such precious fluid in so foolhardy a manner).

"Or," he proclaimed, "are you heathens tempting an innocent child into the ways of the nymph, stirring the wildness in her nature and fomenting the bestial longings in her blood?"

The brunette threw her hands up. "Jesus Christ, Max!"

The musicians were looking at each other like the Three Stooges wondering how to explain their latest botched wallpapering job to their boss. Wide eyes peered out of the drifting cigarette smoke around us as the Renaissance reunion got a good look at the man of the hour, who was dramatically draining the whiskey glass, handing the empty vessel to the nearest bewildered musician.

Then, moving with unexpected quickness, and force, Bodenheim grabbed the woman by the arm and she squealed with pain as he intoned, "Or is this 'innocent' the heathen? If we are to believe Schopenhauer, women are incapable of romantic love, yet infinitely capable of unfathomable treachery ..."

"Excuse me," I told the horrified but spellbound Marilyn, and got up and put my hand on Bodenheim's shoulder.

"It is rather unfortunate," he was saying, still clutching his wife's arm, his face inches from hers with its wide eyes and lips drawn back in snarl, "that the legs of a girl cannot be nailed to the floor.... It's hard to keep them in one place, except when they are locked up in closets."

I said, "Been a long time, Max."

The rheumy blue eyes tried to focus, and he suddenly noticed the hand on his shoulder, looking down at it as if it were an oversize, unpleasant moth that had landed there. "I don't know you, young man. Kindly remove your meat hook from my shoulder."

I did, then extended my hand. "Nate Heller. Mahlon's son."

A wrinkled smile formed under the lumpy nose and the eyes tightened in remembrance. "Heller's Books. Ah yes. The West Side. Wonderful days. Days of youth and passion."

Ric, just behind us, was rounding up his musicians and herding them out of the bar and back up into the dining room.

In the meantime, Bodenheim had unhanded the brunette and was gesturing to her rather grandly with his corncob pipe in hand. "Heller's Books, allow me to introduce Mrs. Maxwell Bodenheim."

The pretty, lanky lush smiled at me, looked me up and down with open appreciation, and said, "I'll have to get Max to bring me to Chicago more often."

"You'll have to forgive Ruth," Bodenheim said, his smile tightening. "She has the morals of an alley cat, but she can't help it. She, too, comes from a newspaper background ..."

"You mean like *me*, Max?" Ben asked, stepping into our rarefied social circle. He had a cigar in the fingers of the hand that held his glass of Scotch. He had the uneasy smile of a host who suddenly realized he had invited a disaster area for a guest.

Bodenheim beamed at the sight of his old friend and adversary; his smile had more holes than teeth. "I was referring ..." He gestured and sneered and stage-whispered: " ... to these lesser lights. Literary section editors. Book reviewers. Columnists...."

Ben smirked. "Try not to alienate them too bad, Bodie, till I pass the hat for ya."

Ruth floated off and I returned to the small table where a stilted Marilyn was talking to Herb Lyon of the *Trib*. He was trying to wrangle an impromptu follow-up interview for his Tower Ticker column; I gently let Herb know this was a social occasion and he drifted off. Soon Marilyn was sipping a glass of champagne; I had a Coke—I was working, after all—while Bodenheim (who had somehow acquired another drink) had Hecht up against a wall, the former getting worked up and Hecht's patient smile wearing thinner and thinner.

I only got bits and pieces of it, mostly Bodenheim, saying, "I have always liked your work, my cynical friend, I can honestly say I've never slammed it ... *Count Bruga*, of course, excepted.... Ben, you had great ability in fields of prose, where money alone lies. I am an indifferent prose writer and a very good poet. That explains the difference in our purses!"

"Such a sad, brilliant man," Marilyn said, working on her second glass of champagne.

"Sad, anyway."

"You don't think he's brilliant?"

"He's got an impressive line of bullshit," I said, "for a deadbeat."

"How can you say that? His language is beautiful!"

"But what he says is ugly."

"I don't care. I want to meet him."

I didn't argue with her. Mine was not to reason why. Mine was but to do and sigh.

As I approached Bodenheim, he continued filibustering his old friendly foe: "If we don't raise at least twenty dollars tonight, Ben, I shan't be able to get my typewriter out of hock when I return to that shallow, mean, and uncouth frenzy known as New York."

"Then as you wend your way around this room, Bodie," Ben said, smiling the world's tightest smile, "I suggest you find some topic of discussion beside the 'stench of Capitalism.' Your old friends, the ones still alive anyway, aren't radicals anymore. They're democrats."

"I do need my typewriter," Bodenheim said, as if Ben had said nothing, "even though I have not sold one of my short stories or poems yet this year." He took a healthy swig from his latest glass of whiskey. "But hope is a warmly smiling, stubbornly tottering child—and without a typing machine I would feel like a writer with spinal meningitis."

I whispered to Ben: "Marilyn wants to meet the Great Man."

Ben rolled his eyes, and said, "All right, but let's both chaperone him, then."

Bodenheim was saying, "You might consider it a persecution complex, but I'm convinced these rejections stem from the days when I threw many a caustic jab at the intellectual dwarfs who pass as literary editors and critics ..."

Taking his toothpick arm, I said, "Max, that lovely blonde would like to meet you. She's quite famous. That's Marilyn Monroe."

"Heller Books, it would be my immense pleasure!" he said, something flickering in the cloudy eyes, the ghost of a once-great womanizer, perhaps.

I ushered him over to the table, where Marilyn rose, smiling, almost blushing, saying, "Mr. Bodenheim, I've worn my copy of your *Selected Poems* simply to tatters."

He took her hand and, much as Ric had, kissed it; I hope she washed it, later. With antiseptic soap.

"My dear," Bodenheim said, bowing, "your taste is as impeccable as your skin is luminous. May I sit?"

She gestured eagerly. "Please."

Ben and I commandeered a couple extra chairs and the four of us crowded around the postage-stamp table as the Tattered King of Greenwich Village conferred with Hollywood's reigning Sex Queen.

"Miss Monroe, I have admired your contributions to the cinema," he said.

"I would think an artist of your stature wouldn't find much of value in what I do," she said, obviously as flattered as she was surprised.

Ben said, "I never knew you to go to a picture show, Bodie."

"I have slept in some of the finest grindhouses on Forty-Second Street," he said rather grandly. He was looking around, probably for his wife. She was nowhere in sight. He returned his gaze to the incandescent beauty who hung on his every word.

"I adore your contribution to the arts, my dear," he said, the sarcasm so faint I wasn't sure it was there. "You remind me of the Bali woman who walks naked down to her navel, and proudly displays her beautifully formed breasts; making love is as a natural to her as breathing, or singing. Sex is really the song of the spirit as well as the flesh, and my dear, you are a prima donna, a diva, of your art."

This slice of condescension-laced sexual innuendo made Ben wince, but Marilyn seemed not to mind, even to take it as a compliment.

"But what I do is so ... ephemeral," Marilyn said. "Your poetry will live forever."

He leaned forward. "Do you know what poetry is, my dear?"

"I think I do ... I don't know if I could put it into words ..."

Now he sat back again. "It's the deep, unformed longing to escape from daily details ... to enter delicately imaginative plateaus, unconnected with human beliefs, or fundamental human feelings ..."

"Oh, but Mr. Bodenheim ..."

He puffed the corncob. "Call me Max, child—or Bodie, as my friends do."

Ben rolled his eyes, as if to say, *What friends?*

Marilyn's expression was heartbreakingly sincere. "But, Max ... your poems are *filled* with human feeling...."

He nodded, exhaling foul smoke; I had a hunch if you took the smoke away, he wouldn't smell much better.

"I am cursed with a malady of the soul," the poet said. "I am constantly tempted to desert the sleek jest of this physical existence."

Her eyes tightened. Her question was a whisper: "Suicide?"

"My life has been a dirty, cruel, involved, crucified mess— with the exception of my glittering words. And sometimes I even hate them, my pretty, glittering words. But where would I be without that golden braid of language that lifts me up out of my life?"

"Would you ... would you ever do it? Take your own life?"

"I think not, child. We demonstrate the truth or falsity of our lives by the manner of our deaths."

"What do you mean?"

"Those who die in a tavern brawl like Christopher Marlowe or in a fit of desperation like Hart Crane leaping off a ship in mid-ocean reveal in their violent deaths the inadequate inner workings of their secret beings.... Are you familiar with this one?

I shall walk down the road.

I shall turn and feel upon my feet

The kisses of Death, like scented rain."

"For Death is a black slave with little silver birds," Marilyn said, *"perched in a sleeping wreath upon his head."*

"You do me great honor," Bodenheim said, touching a hand to his chest, lowering his head, then chugging some whiskey.

"So many of your poems are about death ... and love."

"I am a man, and man is human, all too human, placed by the theologians a little below the angels. Life is the struggle between the pull of the divine and the downward drag of the beast."

She was leaning forward, rapt in the wise man's words. "Is suicide divine, or beastly?"

"Neither. Both. Perhaps I'll answer your question in my next poem." Then he shrugged and began working on relighting his corncob. "But as long as Ruth lives, I'll not take my life."

"Ruth? Your wife?"

"My sweet better half, with whom I share park benches, flophouse suites, and what remains of my tattered existence. We have an exquisite arrangement—she cheats on me, and I beat on her. An inventive girl. Burned down her parents' house, you know. There are those who say that she is mad, but who among us does not have eccentricities?"

"Is she a poet, too?"

He had the corncob going again. "She's a writer."

Marilyn swallowed, summoned bravery and said, "I write poetry."

His smile was benevolent. "You do, my child?"

"Would you like to hear one?" She smiled. "I think I've had enough champagne to get the nerve ...

Life—I am of both your directions
Somehow remaining
Hanging downward the most
Strong as a cobweb in the wind ..."

"You wrote that?"

"Yes."

Bodenheim shook his head. "Sentimental slush." He stood suddenly. "Stick to the silver screen, sweetie."

And he rose and stumbled off into the crowd.

Marilyn had turned a ghostly white, her mouth slack, her face without expression, her eyes wide and vacant and yet filled with pain.

Ben touched her arm and said, "Marilyn, I'm sorry ... he's a drunken no-good bastard. Hell, he thinks *Ezra Pound* stinks...."

"Nathan ... could you please take me back to the hotel?"

"Sure."

But Marilyn was already up and moving out, and I was working to keep up with her. She didn't begin crying until we were in back of the cab, and I held her in my arms and comforted her, telling her how much I liked her poem.

At the door of her suite, I said, "He's a Skid Row bum, you're a goddess. They'll be watchin' your movies when this guy's poems turn to dust."

She smiled, just a little, and touched my face with the gentlest hand imaginable.

Then she kissed me.

Sweetly. Sadly.

"Do you want me to come in?" I asked.

"Next time, Nathan," she said.

And sealed herself within.

3

I met Ben for lunch at the Pump Room at the Ambassador East. It was an atmosphere perfect for Marilyn Monroe—deep blue walls, crystal chandeliers, white leather booths, waiters in English Regency attire serving food elegantly from serving carts and off flaming swords.

But the only celebrities in the room were local newspapermen—fewer than last night at Riccardo's, actually—and, of course, Ben Hecht and that celebrated "private eye to the stars," Nathan Heller.

"She flew out this morning," Ben said, his bloodshot eyes matching the Bloody Mary he was drinking. His second.

"When was she supposed to leave?"

"Not until late this afternoon. We were going to meet with the Doubleday people after lunch."

"Hope your book deal didn't get queered."

"Nah. I'll meet with Marilyn back in Hollywood, it'll be fine. How would you like to bodyguard her again?"

"Twist my arm."

"You two seemed to hit it off."

"I kept it businesslike."

"You mean, that fucking Bodie queered it for you."

I grinned, sipped my rum and Coke. "Bingo."

"Well, Doubleday wants Marilyn to make an appearance at next year's ABA, kicking off a promotional tour for the book. If

I can talk her into it, which I think I can, I'll toss the security job A-1's way."

"I appreciate that, Ben. Maybe I'll let you ghost my autobiography."

"Write your own damn book." He laughed hollowly; he looked terrible, dark bags, pallid complexion, second chin sagging over his crisp blue bow tie. "Guess how much we raised for Bodie last night?"

"Five bucks?"

"Oh, much more ... twelve."

I chuckled at this pleasant bad news. "He must have got even cuter after I left, to get such an overwhelming acclamation."

Ben's smirk made the fuzzy caterpillar of his mustache wriggle. "He caught his wife coming on to a waiter and started screaming flowery obscenities at her and finally slapped her face. When Ric stepped between them, Ruth slapped him and started shouting, 'I'm Mrs. Maxwell Bodenheim! I'm Mrs. Maxwell Bodenheim!'" He sighed and shook his head and sipped his Bloody Mary. "I think Max may have made the record books on this one—the only guy in history ever to get thrown out of his own benefit party."

"He's a horse's ass. What possessed you to fly him and his harpy out here, anyway?"

He didn't answer the question; instead he said, "That was awful, how he crushed that poor kid, last night. Little Marilyn may be built like a brick shithouse, but she's delicate, you know, underneath that war paint."

"I know. I'd have knocked the bastard's teeth out, if he had any."

Ben snorted a second to that motion, finished his Bloody Mary, and waved a waiter over, telling him we'd have another round before we ordered lunch.

"Don't be too tough on Bodie," Ben said. "Language and a sense of superiority are all he has. He doesn't have money to eat or buy clothes, just words he can use to make other people feel like they're bums, too."

"He's just a mean old drunk."

Ben shook his head, smiling grimly. "Problem is, kid, there's a young man in that old skin. He lives in sort of a child's world filled with word toys. He's a poet who lives in a world of poetry ..."

"He's a stumblebum who lives in the gutter."

The waiter brought Ben's third Bloody Mary. Ben stared into the drink, as if it were a crystal ball into his past. His voice was hushed as he said: "We made a sort of pact, Bodie and I, back when we were young turks, cynical sentimental souls devoted to Art." A sudden grin. "Ever hear about the time we spoke at this pompous literary society for a hundred bucks? Which was real cabbage in those days ..."

"Can't say I have."

"We agreed to put on a full-scale literary debate on an important topic. The hall was full of these middle-class boobs, this was in Evanston or someplace, and I got up and said, 'Resolved: that people who attend literary debates are imbeciles. I shall take the affirmative. The affirmative rests.' Then Bodie got up and said, 'You win.' And we ran off with the hundred."

I waited till Ben's laughter at his own anecdote let up before saying, "So you grew up and made some real money, and Peter Pan flew to the gutter. So what?"

Ben sighed again. "I was hoping last night we'd raise some real money for the son of a bitch ..."

"Why?"

"Because, goddamnit, I've been supporting him for fucking *years*! He'd send me sonnets and shit, in the mail, and I sent him two hundred bucks a month. Only, I can't afford it anymore! Not since my career hit the fan."

"You got no responsibility to underwrite that bum."

"Not any more, I don't. Fuck that toothless sot." He opened the menu. "Let's order. I'm on expense account with Doubleday...."

4

I had every reason to expect I'd seen and heard the last of Maxwell Bodenheim, and his lovely souse of a spouse, and to take Ben Hecht at his word, that he was finished with subsidizing the bard of Skid Row.

But the first week of February, at the office, I got a call from Ben.

"You want to do another job for me, kid?"

"If it involves Marilyn Monroe."

"It doesn't, really. Unless you consider it an extension of what you did for me, before. Did you hear what happened to Bodenheim, after the party at Riccardo's?"

"You told me," I reminded him. "He and the missus got tossed out on their deserving backsides."

"No, I mean after that. Remember how I told you we raised a grand total of twelve bucks for him?"

"Yeah."

"Well, he spent it on rubbing alcohol. He was found in the gutter the next morning, beaten to shit, with half a bottle of the stuff clutched in his paws."

"Mugged?"

"I doubt it. More like he'd been mouthing off and got worked over for it."

"This didn't make the papers or I'd know about it."

"See, you don't know everything that goes on in Chicago, kid. Even out in Hollywood, I know more about the town than you ... I got a call from Van Allen Bradley."

Bradley was literary editor over at the *Daily News*. He continued: "Seems the lovely Mrs. Bodenheim, Ruth, came around begging for a book review assignment for Max, so they could raise bus fare back to New York."

"Ben, don't tell me you flew 'em out *one-way*, for that benefit?"

"Hell, yes! I expected to raise a couple thousand for the no-good son of a bitch. How did I know he was going to disintegrate in public?"

"Yeah, who woulda guessed that?"

"Anyway, Bradley assigned some new collection of Edna Vincent Millay, and Ruth brought the review in a day or so later. Bradley says it was well written enough, but figures Ruth wrote it, not Bodie. She stood there at Bradley's desk till he coughed up the dough."

"They're a class act, the Bodenheims."

"Listen, Heller, do you want the job?"

"What is it?"

"In June, back at the ABA, I talked to an editor with a low-end paperback house, about reprinting some of Bodie's books—you know, that racy stuff about flappers fucking? Slap on cover paintings of sexy babes and Bodie's back in business. I got nearly two thousand in contracts lined up for him, which is big money for him."

"So what do you need me for? Just send him the damn contracts."

"Nate, I can't find the SOB. He's a goddamn street bum, floating somewhere around Greenwich Village, or the Bowery.

I know for a while he was staying at this farm retreat on Staten Island, for down-and-outers, run by Dorothy Day, with the *Catholic Worker*? I had a letter from him from there, and I called Dorothy Day and she said Ruth and Bodie showed up on her doorstep, with his arm and leg in a cast from that beating he took. He was there for several months, healing up, and I guess he even managed to sell a poem or two, to the *New York Times*, if you can believe it, for I guess ten bucks apiece ... but Ruth started flirting with some of the male 'guests,' and once his leg healed, Bodie dragged his blushing bride back into the city."

"I'll line up a man in New York to handle it for you, Ben. It'll be cheaper."

"No, Nate—I want *you* to do this. Yourself. You got some history with Bodie; you might get through to him where somebody else wouldn't."

"This could end up costing you more than these contracts are worth."

"Hey, I had a little upturn. I can afford it. I want to get some money to Bodie without gettin' back in the routine of me supportin' him. Anyway, I think it would do him good to see his work back in print."

I laughed, once. "You really are that bastard's friend."

"He doesn't deserve it, does he?"

"No."

5

The Waldorf Cafeteria, on Sixth Avenue near Eighth Street, was within a stone's throw of MacDougal Alley and its quaint studios and New York's only remaining gas streetlamps, in the midst of one of Greenwich Village's several centers of nightlife. Here, where skyscrapers were conspicuous in their absence, and brick buildings and renovated stables held sway, countless little bistros and basement boîtes had sprung up on the narrow, chaotically arranged streets like so many exotic mushrooms. Longhaired men and shorthaired women wandered in their dark, drab clothes and sunglasses, moving through a lightly falling snow like dreary ghosts.

Finding Maxwell Bodenheim took exactly one afternoon. I had begun at Washington Square, where I knew he had once pinned his poems to a picket fence for the dimes and quarters of tourists. A bearded creator of unframed modernistic landscapes working the same racket for slightly inflated fees informed me that "Mad Max" (as I soon found all who knew him in the Village referred to him) had given up selling art to the tourist trade.

"He got too weird for the room, man," the black-overcoat-clad artiste of perhaps twenty-five told me, between alternating puffs of cigarette smoke and cold-visible breath. "You know, too threatening—half-starved looking and drunk and smelly ... the Elks won't do business with a crazy man."

"The Elks?"

"Out-of-towners, man—you know, Elks and Rotarians and Babbitts. Or cats from Flatbush or the Bronx who let their hair down when they hit Sheridan Square."

"So what's Max up to, now?"

"He's around. Moochin' drinks and peddlin' poems for pennies in bars. Been runnin' the blinkie scam, I heard, with some Bowery cats."

I didn't relish hitting that part of town.

"No idea where he lives?"

"Used to be over on Bleecker, but they got evicted. Him and Ruth got busted for sleepin' on the subway. Didn't have the twenty-five bucks fine and spent the night in the can."

"It's a little cold for doorways and park benches."

He shrugged. "They probably still got enough friends to flop for free, here and there. Just start hittin' the coffeehouses and clubs and somebody'll lead you to him."

"Thanks," I said. "Here's a contribution to the arts." And slipped him a fin.

I started to walk away and the guy called out, "Hey man! Did you check with Bellevue? He's been in and out of there."

"As a nutcase or alcoholic?"

"Take your pick."

I called Bellevue, but Max wasn't currently a guest.

So I hit the streets, which were alive with native bohemians and wide-eyed tourists alike—it was Saturday and the dusting of snow wasn't stopping anybody. I covered a lot of ground in about three hours, entering smoky cellar joints where coffee and cake were served with a side of free verse, stepping around wildly illustrated apocalyptic Bible verses in chalk on the sidewalks outside the gin mills of West Eighth Street, checking out such tourist traps as the Nut Club and Café Society and the Village Barn, gandering briefly at the strippers at Jimmy Kelly's, stopping in at cubbyhole restaurants that advertised "health food" in conspicuously unhealthy surroundings, but eating instead at the Café Royal, which advertised itself as "The Center of Second Avenue Bohemia" and served up a mean apple strudel. The name Maxwell Bodenheim was familiar to many, from the Café Reggio to the White Horse Pub, but at the Village Vanguard, a deadpan waif with her raven hair in a pixie cut told me to try the Minneta Tavern, where I learned that the San Remo Café on MacDougal Street was Mad Max's favorite haunt. But at the San Remo, I was sent on to the Waxworks, as the Waldorf Cafeteria was known to hip locals.

What could have possessed the owners of a respectable, pseudo-elegant chain of cafeterias to open a branch in the heart of Bohemia, a place Maxwell Bodenheim had once dubbed "the Coney Island of the soul"? Its wallpaper yellowed and peeling, its "No Smoking" signs defaced and ignored, its once-gleaming fixtures spotted and dull, its floors dirty and littered, its fluorescent lighting sputtered with electrical shorts even while casting a jaundiced glow on the already-sallow faces of a clientele who had taken this cafeteria hostage, turning it from eating place to meeting place. The clatter of dishes and the ring of the pay-as-you-go cash register provided a hard rhythm for the symphony of egos as poets and painters and actors announced their own genius and denounced the lack of talent in others, while occasionally sipping their dime's worth of coffee while nibbling at sandwiches brought from home, the cheap flats they called "studios."

Holding forth at a small side table was the man himself, decked out in a World War One vintage topcoat over the same shabby suit and food-flecked tie he'd worn to the Renaissance reunion, months ago. On the table, as if a meal set out for him, was a worn bulging leather briefcase. Sitting beside him was Ruth, in the pale yellow dress she'd worn to Riccardo's. Both were smoking—Bodie his corncob with that cheap awful tobacco, Ruth with her elbow resting in a cupped hand, cigarette poised near her lips in a royally elegant chain-smoker posture. To the cups of coffee before them Bodenheim was adding generous dollops from a pint of cheap whiskey.

Bodenheim, of course, was talking, and Ruth was nodding, listening, or maybe half-listening; she sat slumped, looking a little bored.

I bought myself a cup of coffee and walked over to them, and bobbed my head toward one of the two untaken chairs at their table. "Mind if I join you?"

As he slipped the pint back in his topcoat pocket, Bodie's rheumy eyes narrowed in their deep shadowy holes; his lumpy face was the color of tapioca, his cheeks sunken to further emphasize the skull beneath the decaying flesh. Sitting up, pretty Ruth, with her big bedroom eyes, one of which drooped drunkenly, again gave me the once-over, like I was another entrée on the cafeteria serving line.

"My wife and I are having a private conversation," Bodie said acidly, then cocked his head. "Do I know you, sir?"

"Yes," I said, sitting down, "from a long time ago, on the West Side of Chicago. But we ran into each other at Riccardo's last June."

The thin line of a mouth erupted into a ghastly array of brownish teeth and sporadic gaps. "Heller's Books! You accompanied that lovely young actress."

Ruth smirked and snorted derisively, as if compared to her Marilyn Monroe was nothing. Smoke came from her nostrils like dragon's breath.

"Yes," I said, "the lovely young actress you humiliated and sent from the room in tears."

He waved that off with a mottled hand. "That was for that sweet child's benefit. Cruelty was the kindest gift I could give her."

"You think?"

"I know." He patted the bulging briefcase before him. "*This* is poetry, my poetry, not sentimental drivel, but the work of a serious artist, a distinguished outcast in American letters—hated and feared, an isolated wanderer in the realm of intellect. If I were to encourage the amateurs, the dilettantes, even ones like Miss Monroe, whose skin shimmers like pudding before the spoon goes in, I would lessen both myself and them."

Ruth cocked her head toward me, rolled her eyes, then winked. She was pretty cute, for a drunk; but I would have had to be pretty drunk, to want to get cute.

"What's your name?" Ruth asked. Her eyes added "Big Boy."

"Nate Heller."

"You're from Chicago? What brings you to the Village?"

"Ben Hecht asked me to look your husband up."

That got Bodenheim's attention and elicited a bitter smirk. "Does my ex-friend wish me to make another cross-country pilgrimage for a twelve-dollar stipend?"

"He's got a publisher interested in reprinting some of your sex books."

Ruth's eyes sobered up and her smile turned from randy to greedy. But the crooked thin line under Bodenheim's sweet-potato nose was curling into a sneer.

"My novels may indeed be inferior to my poetry—I am nothing if not brutally honest with myself where my literary prowess is concerned—but they are hardly 'sex books.' They are not gussied-up pornography, like Hecht's *Fantazius Mallare*. Despite certain flaws, those novels sparkle with social satire and a genuine—"

"Whatever they sparkle with," I said, "there's a publisher willing to pony up a couple grand for the privilege of putting naked women on the covers."

Ruth's eyes were dancing with dollar signs, but Bodenheim was scowling.

"The last time I allowed a cheap pulp publisher ... when was it, five years, eight years ago? ... they bowdlerized the text, even while presenting my work with the sort of sensational gift-wrapping to which you refer. I won't have my work simultaneously exploited *and* censored!"

I leaned forward. "I don't know anything about that. I would guess the last thing this publisher would want to do is trim the dirty parts. So I wouldn't worry about your literary integrity."

Bodenheim froze, his sneering smile dissolving into a hurt, surprised near-pout. "Why, Heller's Books—you don't like me, do you?"

"I wasn't paid to like you. I was paid to find you, and deliver this message." I patted my chest. "I've got the contracts in my inside pocket, if you want me to leave 'em with you. The publisher's right here in New York, you can talk with them, direct. Ben doesn't want any finder's fee, he just wants to see you make a buck or two off your 'prowess.'"

"I don't understand who you are," Bodenheim said, bewildered, the murky eyes suddenly those of a hurt child.

"I'm a private detective."

"I thought you were a literary man ... your father ..."

"Ran a bookstore. Me, like the man says on TV, I'm a cop. In business for myself, but a cop."

"You deal in violence," Bodenheim said quietly.

"Sometimes."

Now a look of sadistic superiority gripped the ravaged face. He leaned forward, gesturing with the foul-smelling corncob. "Are you aware, Heller's Books, of the close connection between the art of murder and the murder of art?"

"I can't say as I am."

"Artists are not killed overnight. They are murdered by being kept alive, as poverty, the unseen assassin, exacts from them one last full measure of agony."

"Is that right."

"When the arts go down to destruction, the artist perishes with them. For some of us, who do not sell our souls to Mammon, the final resting place is Potter's Field. For others it is Hollywood."

"Ben's just trying to help you out, old man. Why in hell, I don't know."

"Why?" Fire exploded in those cloudy eyes. "Because I am the closest thing to a conscience that Ben *Hack*'t has or ever *will* have."

I snorted a laugh. "What do you use for a conscience, old man?"

He settled back into the chair and the eyes went rheumy again; he collapsed into himself and said, very quietly, "My own crushed life sits beside me, staring with sharp, accusing eyes, like a vengeful ghost seeking retribution for some foul murder committed at a time of delirium and terror."

"I don't mean to barge in," a male voice said.

He was a good-looking kid in well-worn jeans and a short-sleeve, slightly frayed white shirt; he had the open face, wide smile, dark-blond pompadour and boyish regular features of the young Buster Crabbe; same broad shoulders, too, only he wasn't as tall, perhaps five eight at most. He only seemed clean-cut at first glance: then I noticed the scars under his left eye and on his chin, and how that wide smile seemed somehow ... wrong.

"Joe," Ruth said warmly, "sit down! Join us."

"This is something of a business discussion," Bodenheim said, tightly.

"Don't be silly, Bodie," she said. "Sit down, Joe."

Joe sat down, next to me, across from Ruth. He was eyeing me suspiciously. I would have sworn the kid was looking at me through the eyes of a jealous boyfriend, but that would be impossible. After all, Ruth was married....

"Joe Greenberg," he said, offering his hand, wearing that big smile, though the eyes remained wary.

"Nate Heller," I said. His handshake let me know just how strong he was.

Bodenheim said, "Mr. Greenberg is a dishwasher here at the Waxworks. It's a career he's pursued with uncommon distinction at numerous establishments around the Village."

"Nice to meet you, Joe," I said. "If you'll excuse me, I was just going ..."

I began to rise but Ruth touched my arm. "Stay for just a little while. Joe, Mr. Heller has wonderful news. A publisher wants to bring some of Max's books back out."

Joe's grin managed to widen, and words streamed out: "Why, Max, that's wonderful! This is a dream come true, I couldn't be happier for—"

"It is not wonderful," Bodenheim said. "It is, like you, Joseph, possibly well-meaning but certainly insulting."

"Max, don't say that," Joe said. "You and Ruth are the best friends I have around here."

"Look," I said, "do you want me to leave the contracts or not?"

"My old friend Ben is not aware," Bodenheim said, with strained dignity, ignoring Joe, who was looking quickly from husband to wife to intruder (me), "that I am currently engaged in the writing of my memoirs for Samuel Roth, publisher of Bridgehead Books."

"That's swell," I said. "Sorry to have bothered you ..."

Again, I began to rise and Ruth stopped me, her brown eyes gazing up, pitifully beseeching. "Mr. Heller, what my husband says is true, he's been going in and writing every day, but the pay is meager. We don't have enough to even put a roof over our heads ... we've been sleeping in doorways, and it's a cold winter ..."

Bodie seemed to be pulling down pay sufficient to afford whiskey.

Joe leaned forward, chiming in, "I told you, Ruth—you and Max are welcome to stay with me ..."

Now it was Ruth leaning forward; she touched Joe's hand. "That's sweet, Joe, but you just have that one small room ... it's an imposition on you ..."

Joe squeezed her hand, then with his other hand stroked it, petted it. His mouth was moist; so were his eyes. "I'd love to have you stay with me ..."

"Leave her alone," Bodenheim spat, "or I'll kill you!"

Joe removed his hand and his face fell into a puttylike expressionless mask. "You hate me, don't you?"

"Of course I do," Bodenheim said, and withdrew his pint and refilled his coffee cup.

"What if I let you two take my room," Joe said nobly, "and me move in with my friend, Allen."

And he nodded toward a skinny redheaded busboy with glasses and pimples who was clearing a table across the room.

"I'll pay the rent," Joe said, "and when you get on your feet, and get your own place, I'll move back in."

"I once warned a girl named Magda," Bodenheim said as if latching onto a stray thought just floating by, "against the possibility of falling into the hands of some degenerate in whom the death of love and the love of death had combined into a homicidal mania. She was strangled in a hotel bed."

Joe was shaking his head. "What are you talkin' about? I'm tryin' to be *nice*...."

Ruth said, "Oh, Bodie, don't you see? Joe's our friend. Don't say such cruel things."

"Today," Bodie said, patronizingly, "when the world is falling apart like scattered beads from a pearl necklace that once graced the lovely throat of existence, the bestial side of man's nature is revealing itself ... blatantly."

"Now *you're* insulting *me!*" Joe said. "I know when I'm being insulted."

"The indignation of fools," Bodenheim said grandly, "is my crown."

I'd had enough of this touching scene. I got up, saying, "I'm in town till Monday. At the Lexington. If you change your mind, Max, give me a call."

As I left, Joe moved around to where I was sitting, nearer to Ruth, and he was leaning forward, speaking quickly, flashing his most ingratiating smile and issuing the best words he could muster, about how his good intentions were being misinterpreted, while Bodenheim sat uncharacteristically silent, frozen with contempt, a sullen wax figure in the Waxworks cafeteria.

6

By the time I got back to my hotel, a message from Max was waiting at the front desk. It had been written down faithfully by the hotel operator: "Mr. Heller—my lovely companion has convinced me to come to my financial senses. Please be so kind as to bring the book contracts tomorrow afternoon between 3 and 4 o'clock to the following address—97 3rd Avenue, near 13th Street. Fifth floor, room 5D."

I showed the desk clerk the address. "Where is that?"

"Lower Fifth Avenue," said the clerk, a boy in his twenties wearing a mustache to look older. "Pretty rough neighborhood. On the fringe of the Bowery."

So I was going to make it to the Bowery, after all. What trip to New York would be complete without it?

I spent the rest of the evening in the Lexington bar making the acquaintance of a TWA stewardess, the outcome of which is neither germane to this story nor any of your business; we slept in the next morning, had a nice buffet lunch at the hotel, and I took her to Radio City Music Hall, where *How to Marry a Millionaire* was playing, one of those new Cinemascope pictures trying to replace 3-D. My companion was lovely, as were the Rockettes, and Betty Grable and Lauren Bacall; but Marilyn made me ache in so many places. She always would.

My new friend caught a cab to the airport, and I grabbed one to the Bowery, where I asked the cabbie to wait for me with the meter running. He warily agreed, and I entered a shambling five-story tenement that looked to be the architectural equivalent of Maxwell Bodenheim himself.

I went up five flights of spongy, creaky stairs, glad I was wearing a topcoat; the building wasn't heated. A window on the fifth floor offered a sweeping city view, more worthy of a postcard than a dingy rooming house; the Third Avenue El was just below. Apartment 5D was at the end of the hall, on the right, the numbers hammered haphazardly into the wall next to the gray-painted door, which had no knob, simply a padlocked hasp.

There was no answer to my repeated knocks. I considered saying to hell with it—so Bodenheim wasn't here, so what? How reliable was a boozehound like Max, anyway?

Pretty reliable, if money was waiting—and I had the feeling his brown-eyed soul mate wouldn't have missed this appointment if even fifty cents were at stake, let alone several thousand. The tiny hairs on the back of my copper's neck were tingling ... and was it my imagination, or was there a stench coming from that room that drowned out the disinfectant and cooking smells and mildew and generally stale air? An all too familiar stench, worse even than Bodie's corncob pipe....

On the first floor I found the pudgy, fiftyish, groundhog-pussed operator ("Not the super! I'm the lessee! The operator!") of this grand hotel. His name was Albert Luck, which was something his tenants were all down on.

"So you know this guy in 5D?" Luck demanded, just outside his door, squinting behind thick-lensed wireframes as if my face were tiny print he was trying to make out; he wore baggy pants and suspenders over his long johns. "This guy Harold Weinberg, you know him?"

"Sure," I lied.

"Son of a bitch Weinberg sneaks in and out like a goddamn ghost," Luck said. "I can't never catch him, and he padlocks the place behind him. If you're such a friend of his, maybe you wanna pay his goddamn rent for him. He's behind two weeks!"

"How much?"

"Ten bucks."

"Five a week?"

He nodded. "Five's the weekly rate; it's eighty-five cents a night."

"I'll pay the back rent," I said, "if you give me a look around in there."

"Can't. It ain't my padlock on the door."

I showed him a sawbuck. "Wouldn't take much to pop the hasp."

"Make it twenty," he said, groundhog eyes glittering, "to cover repairs."

Soon I was following him up the stairs; he wore a plaid hunter's jacket and was carrying a claw hammer and a heavy screwdriver. "Tenants like your friend I don't need.... This ain't a flophouse, you know. These are furnished rooms."

It took him two tries to pop the latch off. I let him open the door, just in case it was a situation where I wouldn't want to be leaving any fingerprints.

It was.

The blood splashed around in the eight-by-nine-foot cubicle was mostly on one wall, and the ceiling above, and on the nearby metal folding cot, and of course on the body of the woman sprawled there on her stomach, still clad in the frayed yellow dress, splotched brown now, the same dried-blood brown that, with the smell of decay, indicated she had been dead some time; this happened at least this morning, maybe even last night.

She had been stabbed in the back, on the left, four times, over her heart and lungs, deep wounds, hunting-knife-type wounds, and from the amount of blood that had soaked her dress and painted the wall and ceiling with an abstraction worthy of Washington Square's outdoor art displays, I figured an artery had been hit. Another slash, on her upper left arm, indicated an attempt to ward off a blow. Her face was battered, bloodied, and blue-gray with lividity.

"Sweet lord Jesus," Albert Luck said. "Who are they?"

"That's Ruth Bodenheim," I said, and then I pointed at the other body. "And that's her husband, Maxwell."

Max was on the floor, on his back, feet near his wife's head where it and its ponytail hung down from the side of the bed. The poet's eyes were wide, seeing nothing, his mouth open and, for once, silent, the flesh as slack on his dead face as if it were melting wax; he had been shot in the chest, a small crusty blossom of brown and black on his dingy white shirt, bloodstain mingled with powder burns, near his tattered tie. His loose black suit coat was on, unbuttoned, open, and his arms were spread as if he were trying to fly, a sleeve torn and bloody with an apparent knife gash. A book lay near him: *The Sea Around Us* by Rachel Carson; his reading had been interrupted by his killing.

"I better call the cops," Luck said, his eyes huge behind the magnified lenses.

"Keep your shirt on, pops," I said, taking a look around.

A small table near the bed, slightly splashed with blood, had the empty pint bottle of whiskey and a wine bottle with a label that said Blackberry; also, a pad and pencil and some scribbled lines of poetry obscured by blood spatter. A window nearby opened on an airshaft. On a small electric stove sat a three-gallon pot of beans, cold; resting nearby was Bodie's corncob pipe and a half-eaten bagel.

In one corner was Bodenheim's worn leather briefcase, the repository of his art; leaned up against it was a tool of a more recent trade: a crudely lettered beggar's sign saying, I AM BLIND.

No sign of a gun, or a knife.

"I'm callin' the cops," Luck said.

"What does this Harold Weinberg look like?"

Luck frowned. "He's *your* friend."

I gave him a hard look. "Refresh my memory."

The landlord shrugged, said, "Good-lookin' kid, pile of greasy hair, talks too much, smiles too much."

I touched under my left eye, then pointed to my chin. "Scars, here and here?"

"That's him."

I got my wallet out and handed him a C-note. "I wasn't here, understand? The rent was overdue and you got fed up and popped the latch, found them like this."

Luck was nodding as he slipped the hundred in his pants. "Okay by me, mister."

My cab was still waiting.

"What scenic part of the city do want to view next?" the cabbie asked.

"The Waldorf."

"Astoria?"

"Cafeteria. Near MacDougal Alley."

7

Late Sunday afternoon at the Waxworks was pretty slow: a sprinkling of hipsters, a handful of civilians catching an early supper or a slice of pie before heading back to the real world after a few hours in Little Bohemia.

The skinny redheaded busboy, whose horn-rimmed glasses were patched at the bridge with adhesive tape, his pimples mingling with freckles to create a Jackson Pollock canvas, was taking a break, slouched in a chair propped against a wall, smoking beneath a NO SMOKING sign decorated with cigarette burns. He had the gawky, geeky look of a teenager having a hard time with puberty; but on closer look he was probably in his midtwenties, and he had a tattoo of a hula girl on his thin right forearm. His busboy's tray was on the table before him like a grotesque meal.

I sat down beside him and he frowned, irritably, but said rather politely, "You want this table, mister?"

"No, Allen," I said, and smiled, "I want to talk to you."

His eyes, which were a sickly green, narrowed. "How do you know me?"

"Friend of a friend."

"What friend?"

"Joe Greenberg. Or do you know him as Harold Weinberg?"

He swallowed nervously, almost lost his balance in his propped-back chair; righting it, he sat forward. "Joe just works here is all. He's off right now."

"He's off, all right. You wouldn't happen to know where I could I find him?"

Another swallow. He started drumming his fingers on the table and he didn't look at me as he said, tremulously, "No. I ain't seen him today. You try his flop?"

"Matter of fact, yeah. He wasn't there."

"Oh, well ..."

"Two friends of his were. Dead ones."

The eyes locked right onto me now; he was surprised, genuinely surprised—these murders were news to him.

"Oh, didn't he mention that, Allen? That he killed two people? Maybe you knew 'em—Max Bodenheim and his wife Ruth. Good customers."

The ruddy flesh around the pimples and freckles got pale. "Hell. Shit."

"If you're letting him hole up at your place, Allen, you're putting yourself in line for an accessory to murder rap."

His lips were quivering. "Jesus Christ. Jesus Christ.... Are you a cop?"

"Private. I was hired to find Bodenheim on a business matter. I don't want to get involved any more than you do."

His voice lowered to a whisper; what he said was like a profane prayer: "Shit ... I gotta get him out of there!"

Sometimes it pays to play a hunch.

"Allen, let's help each other out on this...."

In 1954, I was licensed in five states to carry firearms in the course of my business, and New York was one of them. I had learned long ago that while my need for a weapon was infrequent, traveling naked could be a chilly proposition; after all, even the most innocuous job had the potential to turn ugly.

So, after a detour back to the Lexington to pick up my nine millimeter and shoulder harness, I took a cab to the address Allen Spiegel had given me: 311 East 21st, near Second Avenue. Joe/Harold had come up in the world, all the way from the bleak Bowery to the godforsaken Gashouse district.

A wind was whipping the remnants of yesterday's snow around in a chilly dust storm. Stepping around a derelict huddling in the doorway, I entered the four-story frame rooming house, a cold, dank breeding ground for cockroaches. Allen was waiting just inside, a frightened host in a shabby sweater and faded jeans.

"The pay phone's on the second floor," he whispered, nodding toward the stairway. "Should I go ahead and call 'em?"

"After you see me go in. It's down that way?"

He nodded and pointed.

"Don't let him see you," I advised.

"Don't worry," he said.

The busboy's room was toward the back of the first floor, with (Allen had informed me) a window that looked out on a backyard that served as a courtyard for adjacent tenements. I glanced around to see if anyone was looking—nobody was but Allen, peeking from beside the stairwell—and I took out my nine millimeter and, with my free hand, knocked.

The voice behind the door was Joe's: "What?"

"Allen sent some food over from the Waxworks," I said. "He thought you might be hungry."

The silence that followed lasted forever. Or was it ten seconds?

Then the door cracked open and I got a sliver of Joe's pasty face before I shouldered my way in, slamming the door behind me, shoving the gun in Joe's face.

"You want to tell me about it, Joe?"

He backed away. He wore a blue work shirt and jeans and he wasn't smiling, anymore; his eyes bore raccoon circles. He didn't have to be told to put up his hands.

The room was no bigger than the one at the other rooming house—another of those "furnished rooms," which is to say a scarred-up table, a couple ancient kitchen chairs, a rusty food-spotted electric stove, unmade Army cot and a flimsy nightstand, fixtures any respectable secondhand store would turn down. The wallpaper was floral and peeling, the floor bare, the window by the bed had no curtains, but a frayed shade was drawn.

On the nightstand was a hunting knife in a black sheath. No sign of a gun.

"You," he said, pointing at me, eyes narrowing, "you're that guy from the Waxworks ..."

"That's right."

"What are you doing here? What are—"

"I had an appointment this afternoon with Max and Ruth. They couldn't keep it, so I'm keeping it with you."

He ventured a facial shrug. "Gee, I haven't seen them since last night at the Waxworks."

"Gee, then how'd they wind up dead in your flop?"

He didn't bother trying to take his lame story any further. He just sat, damn near collapsed, on the edge of the cot. That hunting knife was nearby but he didn't seem to notice it. Anyway, that was what I was supposed to think.

I dragged over a kitchen chair and sat backward on it, leaning forward, keeping the nine millimeter casually trained on him. "What went wrong with your little party, Joe?"

He exploded in a rush of words: "They were just a couple of low-life Communists! Mad Max, hell, he was a walking dead man, and his wife was a common slut! A couple of lousy Reds, through and through!"

"Not to mention inside and out," I said. "When you hit that artery, it must have sprayed like a garden hose."

His eyes widened with the memory I'd just triggered.

"You didn't mean for this to happen, did you, Joe? You just wanted to get laid, right?"

And that wide smile flashed, nervously. "Yeah. Just wanted to tear off a little piece from that gutter-trash quail, like half the fucking Village before me...." The smile turned sideways, and he shook his head. "Shit. She sure was *cute*, wasn't she?"

"How'd it happen, Joe?"

Slumping, staring at nothing, he spoke in the singsongy whine of a child explaining itself: "I thought he fell asleep, reading, the old fart. When he ran out of whiskey, you know, I gave him some wine, and after he drained that, I thought the bastard was out for the night. Or I else wouldn'ta, you know, started fooling around with Ruth on the bed ..."

"Only he woke up and caught you at it."

He shrugged, said, "Yeah, so I took my knife off the table and kind of threatened him with it, told him to get back away from me ... then the old fucker took a *swing* at me ... I think he cut his arm when he did ... and the knife, it kind of went flying."

"What did you shoot him with?"

"I kept this old hunting rifle, .22, next to my bed. That's a rough neighborhood, you know. Bad element."

"No kidding. So you shot him point-blank with the rifle."

Another shrug. "It was self-defense."

"Why did you do the woman, Joe?"

His face tightened with indignation; he pointed to himself with a thumb. "That was self-defense, too! She started screaming and clawing at me, after I shot her old man, so I threw the bitch down the bed, and started just kind of slapping her, you know, just to shut her up, but she wouldn't put a lid on that screaming shit so I hit her a couple times, good ones, only she just yelled louder, and so what the hell else could I do, I grabbed that knife off the floor, and ..."

He stopped, swallowed.

So I finished for him: "Stabbed her in the back four or five times. In self-defense."

That's when he lunged for me, launching himself from the bed and right at me, knocking me and the chair over, ass over teakettle. Then he dove for the knife, but I was up and on him and slammed the nine-millimeter barrel into the back of his hand, crushing it against the nightstand. He yowled and pulled the hand back, shaking it like he'd been burned, and I laid the barrel along the back of his neck, hard, sending him to the floor, where he whimpered like a kicked dog.

I tucked the sheathed knife in my waistband. "Where's your damn rifle?"

"Down ... down a gutter...."

I gave the place a quick toss, looking for the other weapon, or any other weapon, but he was apparently telling the truth. He sat on the floor with his legs curled around under him, like a pitiful little kid who'd just taken a fearsome beating; he was crying, but the eerie thing was, he had that big crazy smile going, too.

"You stay put, Liberace," I said. "I'm calling the cops."

I shut him in there, tucked my gun away, and listened for the sound of the window opening and him clambering out into the courtyard.

It was muffled, but I heard it: "Hold it right there!"

Then a gunshot.

And Joe's voice, pleading: "Please don't kill me! I'll tell you everything!"

Seemed the cops had been waiting when Joe went out that window.

Seemed my friend Allen had spotted a suspicious character in the rooming house hallway, trying various doors, then out back, trying windows, and Allen, being a good citizen, called it in. He thought it might be a fellow he knew from work, a dishwasher named Joe Greenberg with scars on his face and a greasy pompadour, and sure enough, that's who'd been caught, climbing out Allen's window, then trying to scramble over a fence when that cop fired a warning shot. Seemed the police were looking for an individual on a Bowery killing who answered Greenberg's description. Later, a sheathed hunting knife used in the Bowery slaying turned up on the grass by some garbage cans behind Allen's rooming house.

Anyway, that's what the papers said.

How I should I know? I was just the Little Man Who Wasn't There, slipping out the back.

8

Harold Weinberg (Joe Greenberg was an alias) had a history of mental illness, having been first institutionalized at age ten; in 1945, at seventeen, he'd been medically discharged from the Army, and had since racked up a long record of vagrancy and breaking-and-entering arrests. He confessed to the police several times, delivering several variants of what he told me, as well as a version that had Bodenheim killing Ruth and prompting Weinberg to retaliate with the .22, as well as my favorite, one in which a person hiding under the bed did it. Weinberg sang "The Star-Spangled Banner" at his arraignment, bragged about ridding the world of two Communists, assured spectators he was "not crazy," and was promptly committed to Bellevue, where Maxwell Bodenheim and his wife Ruth were also registered, albeit in the morgue.

I claimed the bodies, at Ben Hecht's behest, who shared funeral expenses with Bodenheim's first wife, Minna, subject of Max's first book of poetry. Three hundred attended the poet's funeral, including such leading literary lights as Alfred Kreymborg and Louis Untermeyer, among a dozen other nationally known figures in the arts, who mingled with lowly Village poets, painters, and thespians. Kreymborg gave a eulogy that included the prediction, "We need not worry about Maxwell Bodenheim's future—he will be read."

And Bodenheim's murder did receive enormous national coverage—probably no Bowery bum in history ever got such a send-off—and by dying violently in a sexually charged situation, the one-time bestselling author of *Replenishing Jessica* gained a second fifteen minutes of fame (to invoke a later oddball Village luminary).

But Kreymborg's prediction has otherwise proved less than prescient. Every one of Bodie's books was out of print at his death, and the same is true as I write this, forty-some years later. As far as I'm aware, the last time a Bodenheim book was in print was 1961, when a low-end paperback publisher put some sexy babes on the cover of the Greenwich Village memoirs he was writing at the time of his death.

The body of the former Ruth Fagan was claimed by her family in Detroit.

As I had intended, and done my best to arrange, my participation in the official investigation into the murder of Maxwell Bodenheim and his wife Ruth was minimal; I gave a statement about the argument I'd seen at the Waxworks on the evening of Saturday, February 7. I was not required to testify, and while I'm sure at some point Weinberg must have told the cops about the guy with the automatic who took a confession from him in Allen Spiegel's rooming-house room, it was likely written off as just another of the numerous ravings of a madman who was eventually committed to Matteawan State Hospital for the Criminally Insane; he was released in 1977, and was behind bars again within a year on an attempted murder charge.

Until his death in 1964, Ben Hecht continued to write (and doctor) movie scripts, if with far less distinction than the glory days of the '30s and '40s. His real comeback was as a writer of nostalgic, wry memoirs, including *A Child of the Century* in 1954, in which he waxed fondly of Max; he tended to write of Chicago, not Hollywood or New York, and glorified the Chicago

Renaissance (and himself) whenever possible, never letting the truth stand in the way of a good yarn.

He also completed the Marilyn Monroe "autobiography," which was entitled *My Story*, but the project hit an unexpected snag.

"Looks like I won't be paying you to make goo-goo eyes at Marilyn Monroe at this year's ABA," Ben said to me on the phone, in April of '54.

"Hell you say. Why not? Isn't she making an appearance?"

"Yeah, but not at the ABA. In court. That bimbo's suing me!"

Ben's British agent had peddled the serialization rights to the book overseas, without Marilyn's permission. Her new husband, Mr. DiMaggio, convinced her she was being swindled and, besides, he didn't like the idea of the book, anyway. Ben's agent had violated the agreement with Marilyn, who hadn't signed a final book contract; the book was pulled, the lawsuit dropped. *My Story* wasn't published until 1974, when Marilyn's former business partner, Milton Greene, sold it to Stein and Day, without mentioning Hecht's role.

I did, however, encounter Marilyn again, and in fact had heard from her prior to Ben's news about the busted book project. About a week after Bodenheim's death, when I was back in Chicago, I received a phone call, at home, at three in the morning.

"I'm sorry to call so late," the breathy voice said.

"That's okay ..." I said, sitting up in bed, blinking myself awake, pretty sure I recognized the voice, but thinking I was possibly still dreaming.

"This is Marilyn Monroe. You know—the actress?"

"I think I remember you. Very little gets past me. I'm a trained detective."

She laughed a little, but when the voice returned, it was sad. "I couldn't sleep. I was thinking about what I read in the papers."

"What did you read?"

"About that poor man. Mr. Bodenheim."

"He was cruel to you."

"I know. But life was cruel to him."

We talked for a good hour, about life and death and poetry and her new husband and how happy she was. It was a sweet, sad phone call. Delicate, gentle, poetic in a way that I don't think Maxwell Bodenheim ever was, frankly.

The best thing you can say about Max is that, unlike a lot of writers who hit the skids and the bottle, he never stopped writing. He never stopped filling paper with his poetry.

On the other hand, I think about the sign I found in that ten-by-ten hellhole where he died, the cardboard on which he'd scrawled the words: I AM BLIND.

Probably the truest poem he ever wrote.

STRIKE ZONE

1

My buddy Bill Veeck made many a mark in the world of big league baseball, owning his first club at twenty-eight, winning pennants, setting attendance records. Two of Bill's teams beat the Yankees in their heyday—the '48 Cleveland Indians and the '59 White Sox; only one other team managed that feat, the '54 Indians, which was mostly made up of Veeck's former players.

And, of course, Bill Veeck was a character as colorful as his exploding-paint-factory sport shirts—one of his many trademarks was a refusal to wear coat and tie—a hard-drinking, chain-smoking extrovert with a wooden leg and a penchant for ignoring such quaint customs as doctors' orders and a good night's sleep. Veeck thought nothing of commuting from Cleveland to New York, to hang out with showbiz pals like Frank Sinatra and Skitch Henderson at the Copa, or to fly at the drop of a cap out to Hollywood for a game of charades with Hope and Crosby.

"Baseball is too grim, too serious," he liked to say. "It should be fun. Most owners are bunch of damn stuffed shirts."

Many of Veeck's stunts and promotions and just plain wild ideas indeed had irritated the stuffed shirts of baseball. During World War Two, when the draft had drained the game of so much talent, Veeck told Commissioner Kenesaw Mountain Landis that he planned to buy the Phillies and fill the team with black ballplayers (another buyer was quickly found). Still,

Veeck did manage to put the first black player in the American League, Larry Doby, and even brought the legendary Negro Leagues pitcher, Satchel Paige, into the majors.

Nonetheless, Bill Veeck was resigned to the fact that—no matter what his other accomplishments, whether noble or absurd—he would go down in baseball history as the guy who brought a midget into the majors.

Back in June of '61, when Veeck called the A-1 Detective Agency, saying he had a job for me, I figured it would have something to do with his recent resignation as president of the White Sox. A partner had bought out both Bill and his long-time associate, Hank Greenberg, and I wondered if it'd been a squeeze play.

Maybe Bill needed some dirt dug up on somebody. Normally, at that stage of my career anyway, I would have left such a shabby task to one of the agency's many operatives, rather than its president and founder—both of which were me.

I had known Veeck for something like fifteen years, however, and had done many an odd job for him. And besides, my policy was when a celebrity asked for Nate Heller, the celebrity got Nate Heller.

And Bill Veeck was, if nothing else, a celebrity.

The afternoon was sunny with a breeze, but blue skies were banished in the shadow of the El, where Miller's nestled, an undistinguished Greek-run American-style restaurant that Veeck had adopted as his favorite Loop hangout, for reasons known only to him. Any time Veeck moved into a new office, his first act was to remove the door—another of his trade-marks—and Miller's honored their famous patron by making one of Veeck's discarded doors their own inner front one, with an explanatory plaque, and the inevitable quote: "My door is always open—Bill Veeck."

At a little after three p.m., Miller's was hardly hopping, its dark front windows adding to the under-the-El gloom. Bill was seated in his usual corner booth, his wooden leg extended into the aisle. I threaded through the empty Formica tables and, after a handshake and hello, slid in opposite him.

"Well, you look like hell," I told him.

He exploded with laughter, almost losing his corner-of-the-mouth cigarette. "At last an honest man. Everybody else tells me I look in the pink—I'm getting the same kind of good reviews as a well-embalmed corpse."

Actually, a well-embalmed corpse looked better than Veeck: his oblong face was a pallid repository for pouchy eyes, a long lumpy nose, and that wide, full-lipped mouth, which at the moment seemed disturbingly slack. His skin—as leathery and well-grooved as a catcher's mitt—hung loose on him, and was startlingly white. I had never seen him without a tan. Though I was ten years older, Veeck in his midforties looked sixty. A hard sixty.

"It's a little late to be looking for dirt on Allyn, isn't it?" I asked him, after a waitress brought Veeck a fresh bottle of Blatz and a first one for me.

Arthur Allyn had bought the White Sox and was the new president.

"This isn't about that," Veeck said gruffly, waving it off. "Art's a pal. This sale clears the way for Hank to relocate in LA. When I get feeling better, Hank'll take me in as a full partner."

"Then what is this about, Bill?"

"Maybe I just want to hoist one with you, in honor of an old friend."

"Oh.... Eddie Gaedel. I guess I should have known."

We clinked beer bottles.

I had seen Eddie's obit in yesterday's paper—and the little story the *Trib* ran in sports. Eddie had died of natural causes, the coroner had said, and bruises on his body were "probably suffered in a fall."

"I want you to look into it," Veeck said.

"Into what?"

"Eddie's death."

"Why? If it was natural causes."

"Eddie's mother says it was murder."

I sipped my beer, shook my head. "Well, those 'bruises' could have come from a beating he got, and deserved—Eddie always was a mouthy little bastard. A week after that game in St. Louis, ten years ago, he got arrested in Cincinnati for assaulting a cop, for Christ's sake."

Veeck swirled his beer and looked down into it with bleary eyes—in all the years I'd known this hard-drinking SOB, I'd never once seen him with bloodshot eyes ... before.

"His mother says it's murder," Veeck repeated. "Run over to the South Side and talk to her—if what she says gets your nose twitchin', look into it.... If it's just a grieving mother with some crazy idea about how her 'baby' died, then screw it."

"Okay. Why is this your business, Bill?"

"When you spend six months bouncing back and forth between your apartment and the Mayo Clinic, you get to think-ing ... putting your affairs in order. Grisly expression, but there it is."

"What is it? The leg again?"

"What's left of it. The latest slice took my knee away, finally. That makes seven operations. Lucky seven."

"Semper fi, mac," I said, and we clinked bottles again. We'd both been marines in the South Pacific, where I got malaria and combat fatigue, and he had his leg run over by an antitank gun on the kickback. Both of us had spent more time in hospitals than combat.

"My tour was short and undistinguished," he said. "At least you got the Bronze Star."

"And a Section Eight."

"So I lost half a leg, and you lost half your marbles. We both got a better deal than a lot of guys."

"And you want me to see what kind of deal Eddie Gaedel got?"

"Yeah. Seems like the least I could do. You know, I saw him, not that long ago. He did a lot of stunts for me, over the years. Last year I dressed him up as a Martian and ran him around the park. Opening day this year, I had midget vendors working the grandstand, giving out cocktail wieners in little buns, and shorty beers."

"And Eddie was one of the vendors."

"Yeah. Paid him a hundred bucks—same as that day back in '51."

That day when Eddie Gaedel—3' 7", sixty-five pounds—stepped up to the plate for the St. Louis Browns, batting for Frank Saucier.

"Funny thing is," Veeck said, lighting up a fresh cigarette, "how many times I threatened to kill that little bastard myself. I told him, I've got a man up in the stands with a high-powered rifle, and if you take a swing at any pitch, he'll fire."

"You got the mother's address?"

"Yeah ... yeah, I got it right here." He took a slip of paper out of his sport shirt pocket but didn't hand it to me. "Only she's not there right now."

"Where is she?"

"Visitation at the funeral home. Service is tomorrow morning."

"Why don't I wait, then, and not bother her ..."

The gravel voice took on an edge. " 'Cause I'd like you to represent me. Pay her and Eddie your respects ... plus, your detective's nose might sniff something."

"What, formaldehyde?"

But I took the slip of paper, which had the funeral home address as well as Mrs. Gaedel's.

He was saying, "Do you know the *New York Times* put Eddie's obit on the front page? The front goddamn page.... And that's the thing, Nate, that's it right there: my name is in Eddie's obit, big as baseball. And you know what? You know damn well, time comes, Eddie'll be in mine."

I just nodded; it was true.

The pouchy eyes tightened—bloodshot maybe, but bright and hard and shiny. "If somebody killed that little bastard, Nate, find out who, and why, and goddamnit, do something about it."

I squinted through the floating cigarette smoke. "Like go to the cops?"

Veeck shrugged; his wrinkled puss wrinkled some more. "You're the one pitching. Hurl it any damn way you want to."

2

Of course this had all begun about ten years before—in the summer of '51—when Veeck called me and asked if I knew any midgets who were "kinda athletic and game for anything."

"Why don't you call Marty Craine," I said, into the phone, leaning back in my office chair, "or some other booking agent."

"Marty's come up blank," Veeck's voice said through the long-distance crackle. "Can't you check with some of those lowlife pals of yours at the South State bump-and-grind houses? They take shows out to the carnivals, don't they?"

"You want an athletic midget," I said, "I'll find you an athletic midget."

So I had made a few calls, and wound up accompanying Eddie Gaedel on the train to Cleveland, for some as yet unexplained Bill Veeck stunt. Eddie was in his midtwenties but had that aged, sad-eyed look common to his kind; he was pleasant enough, an outgoing character who wore loud sport shirts and actually reminded me of a pint-size Veeck.

"You don't know what the hell this is about?" he kept asking me in his high-pitched squawk, an oversize cigar rolling from one corner to the other of his undersize mouth.

"No," I said. We had a private compartment and Gaedel's incessant cigar smoking provided a constant blue haze. "I just know Bill wants this kept mum—I wasn't to tell anybody but you, Eddie, that we're going to Cleveland to do a job for the Browns."

"You follow baseball, Nate?"

"I'm a boxing fan myself."

"I hope *I* don't have to know nothing about baseball."

"Veeck didn't say you had to know baseball—just you had to be athletic."

Gaedel was a theatrical midget who had worked in various acrobatic acts.

"Ask the dames," Gaedel said, chortling around the pool-cue Havana, "if Eddie Gaedel ain't athletic."

That was my first clue to Eddie's true personality, or anyway the Eddie that came out after a few drinks. In the lounge car, after he threw back one, then another Scotch on the rocks like a kid on a hot day downing nickel Cokes, I suddenly had a horny Charlie McCarthy on my hands.

I was getting myself a fresh drink, noticing out the corner of an eye as Eddie sidled up to a pair of attractive young women—a blonde and brunette traveling together, probably college students, sweaters and slacks—and set his drink on their little silver deco table. He looked first at the blonde, then at the brunette, as if picking out just the right goodie in a candy-store display case.

Then he put his hand on the blonde's thigh and leered up at her.

"My pal and me got a private compartment," he said, gesturing with his cigar like an obscenely suggestive wand, "if you babes are up for a little four-way action."

The blonde let out a yelp, brushing off Eddie's hand like a big bug. The brunette was frozen in Fay Wray astonishment.

Eddie grabbed his crotch and grinned. "Hey doll, you don't know what you're missin'—I ain't as short as you think."

Both women stood and backed away from the little man, pressing up against the windows, pretty hands up and clawed, their expressions about the same as if a tarantula had been crawling toward them.

I got over there before anybody else could—several men stood petrified, apparently weighing the urge to play Saint George against looking like a bully taking on such a pint-size dragon.

Grabbing him by the collar of his red shirt, I yanked the midget away from the horrified girls, saying, "Excuse us, ladies.... Jesus, Eddie, behave yourself."

And the little guy spun and swung a hard sharp fist up into my crotch. I fell to my knees and looked right into the contorted face of Eddie Gaedel, a demented elf laughing and laughing at the pitiful sight that was me.

A white-jacketed conductor was making his alarmed way toward us when my pain subsided before Eddie's knee-slapping laughter, giving me the window of opportunity to twist the little bastard's arm behind him and drag him out of the lounge, through the dining car, getting lots of dirty looks from passengers along the way for this cruelty, and back to our compartment, tossing him inside like the nasty little rag doll he was.

He picked himself up, a kind of reassembling action, and came windmilling at me, his high-pitched scream at once ridiculous and frightening.

I clipped him with a hard right hand and he collapsed like a string-snipped puppet. Out cold on the compartment floor. Well, if you have to be attacked by an enraged horny drunken midget, better that he have a glass jaw.

He slept through the night, and at breakfast in the dining car apologized, more or less.

"I'm kind of an ugly drunk," he admitted, buttering his toast.

"For Christ's sakes, Eddie, you only had two drinks."

"Hey, you don't have to be friggin' Einstein to figure with my body size, it don't take much. Anyway, I won't tell Mr. Veeck my bodyguard beat the crap out of me."

"Yeah. Probably best we both forget the little incident."

He frowned at me, toast crumbs flecking his lips. "'Little' incident? Is that a remark?"

"Eat your poached eggs, Eddie."

In Veeck's office, the midget sat in a wooden chair with his legs sticking straight out as the Hawaiian-shirted owner of the St. Louis Browns paced excitedly—though due to Bill's wooden leg, it was more an excited shuffle. I watched from the sidelines, leaning against a file cabinet.

Suddenly Veeck stopped right in front of the seated midget and thrust an Uncle Bill Wants You finger in his wrinkled little puss.

"Eddie, how would like to be a big-league ballplayer?"

"Me?" Eddie—wearing a yellow shirt not as bright as the sun—squinted up at him. "I been to maybe two games in my life! Plus, in case you ain't noticed, I'm a goddamn midget!"

"And you'd be the only goddamn midget in the history of the game." Tiny eyes bright and big as they could be, Veeck held up two hands that seemed to caress an invisible beach ball. "Eddie, you'll appear before thousands—your name'll go in the record books for all time!"

Eddie's squint turned interested. "Yeah?"

"Yeah. Eddie, my friend ... you'll be immortal."

"Immortal. Wow. Uh ... what does it pay?"

"A hundred bucks."

Eddie was nodding now—a hundred bucks was even better than immortality.

"So what *do* you know about baseball?" Veeck asked him.

"I know you're supposed to hit the white ball with the bat. And then you run somewhere."

Veeck snatched a little toy bat from his desk; then he crouched over as far as his gimpy leg would allow, and assumed the stance.

"The pitcher's gotta throw that white ball in your strike zone, Eddie."

"What the hell is that?"

"It's the area between the batter's armpits and the top of his knees.... Let's see your strike zone."

Eddie scrambled off the chair and took the toy bat, assuming the position.

"How's that, Mr. Veeck?"

"Crouch more. See, since you're only gonna go to bat once in your career, whatever stance you assume at the plate, that's your natural stance."

Eddie, clutching the tiny bat, crouched. His strike zone was maybe one and a half inches.

Then he took an awkward, lunging swing.

"No!" Veeck said. "Hell, no!"

Eddie, still in his crouch, looked at Veeck curiously.

Veeck put his arm around the little guy. "Eddie, you just stay in that crouch. You just stand there and take four balls. Then you'll trot down to first base and we'll send somebody in to run for you."

"I don't get it."

Veeck explained the concept of a walk to Eddie, whose face fell, his dreams of glory fading.

"Eddie," Veeck said pleasantly, "if you so much as look like you're gonna swing, I'm gonna shoot you dead."

Eddie shrugged. "That sounds fair."

On a hot Sunday in August, a crowd of twenty thousand—the largest attendance the chronically losing Browns had managed in over four years—came out to see Bill Veeck's latest wild stunt. The crowd, which was in a great, fun-loving mood, had no idea what that stunt would be; but as this doubleheader with the Tigers marked the fiftieth anniversary of the American League, the fans knew it would be something more than just the free birthday cake and ice cream being handed out.

Or the opening game itself, which the Browns, naturally, lost.

The half-time show began to keep the implied Veeck promise of zaniness, with a parade of antique cars, two couples in Gay Nineties attire pedaling a bicycle-built-for-four around the bases, and a swing combo with Satchel Paige himself on drums inspiring jitterbugging in the aisles. A three-ring circus was assembled, with a balancing act at first base, trampoline artists at second, and a juggler at third.

Throughout all this, I'd been babysitting Eddie Gaedel in Veeck's office. Gaedel was wearing a Browns uniform that had been made up for Bill DeWitt, Jr., the nine-year-old son of the team's former owner/current advisor. The number sewn onto the uniform was actually a fraction: 1/8; and kid's outfit or not, the thing was tentlike on Eddie.

We could hear the muffled roar of the huge crowd, and Eddie was nervous. "I don't feel so good, Nate."

The little guy was attempting to tie the small pair of cleats Veeck had somehow rustled up for him.

"You'll do fine, Eddie."

"I can't tie these friggin' things! Shit!"

So I knelt and tied the midget's cleats. I was getting a hundred bucks for the day, too.

"These bastards hurt my feet! I don't think I can go on."

"There's twenty thousand people in that park, but there's one whose ass I know I can kick, Eddie, and that's you. Get going."

Soon we were under the stands, moving down the ramp, toward the seven-foot birthday cake out of which Veeck planned to have Eddie jump. Big Bill Durney, Veeck's traveling secretary, helped me lift the midget under the arms, so we could ease him onto the board inside the hollowed section of the cake.

"What the hell am I?" Eddie howled, as he dangled between us. No one had told him about this aspect of his appearance. "A stripper?"

"When you feel the cake set down," I said, "jump out, and run around swingin' and clowning. Then run to the dugout and wait your turn at bat."

"This is gonna cost that bastard Veeck extra! I'm an AGVA member, y'know!"

And we set him down in there, handed him his bat, and covered him over with tissue paper, through which his obscenities wafted.

But when the massive cake was rolled out onto the playing field by two of the fans' favorite Browns, Satch Paige and Frank Saucier, and plopped down on the pitcher's mound, Eddie Gaedel rose to the occasion. As the stadium announcer introduced "a brand-new Brownie," Eddie burst through the tissue paper and did an acrobatic tumble across the wide cake, landing on his cleats nimbly, running to home, swinging the bat all the way, eating up the howls of laughter and the spirited applause from the stands.

Then Eddie headed for the dugout, and the various performers were whisked from the field for the start of the second game. The fans were having a fine time, though perhaps some were disappointed that the midget-from-the-cake might be the big Veeck stunt of the day; they had hoped for more.

They got it.

Frank Saucier was the leadoff batter for the Browns, but the announcer boomed, "For the Browns, number 1/8—Eddie Gaedel, batting for Saucier!"

And there, big as life, so to speak, was Eddie Gaedel, swimming in the child's uniform, heading from the dugout with that small bat still in hand, swinging it, limbering up, hamming it up.

Amazed laughter rippled through the crowd as the umpire crooked a finger at Veeck's manager, Zack Taylor, who jogged out with the signed contract and a carbon of the telegram Veeck had sent major league headquarters adding Eddie to the roster.

By this time I had joined Veeck in the special box up on the roof, where visiting dignitaries could enjoy the perks of a bar and restaurant. Veeck was entertaining a crew from Falstaff Breweries, the Browns' radio sponsors, who were ecstatic with the shenanigans down on the diamond. Newspaper photographers were swarming onto the field, capturing the manager of the Tigers, Red Rolfe, complaining to the umpire, while pitcher Bob Cain and catcher Bob Swift just stood at their respective positions, occasionally shrugging at each other, obviously waiting for this latest Bill Veeck gag to blow over.

But it didn't blow over: after about fifteen minutes of discussion, argument, and just plain bitching, the umpire shooed away the photogs and—with clear reluctance—motioned the midget to home plate.

"Look at the expression on Cain's puss!" Veeck exploded at my shoulder.

Even at this distance, the disbelief on the pitcher's face was evident, as he finally grasped that this joke was no joke: he had to pitch to a midget.

"He can't hurl underhand," Veeck was chortling, "'cause submarine pitches aren't legal. Look at that! Look at Swift!"

The catcher had dropped to his knees, to give his pitcher a better target.

"Shit!" Veeck said. His tone had turned on a dime. All around us, the Falstaff folks were having a gay old time; but Veeck's expression had turned as distressed as Cain's. "Will you look at that little bastard, Nate...."

Eddie Gaedel—who Veeck had spent hours instructing in achieving the perfect, unpitch-to-able crouch—was standing straight and, relatively speaking, tall, feet straddled DiMaggio-style, tiny bat held high.

"Have you got your gun, Nate? That little shit's gonna swing...."

"Naw," I said, a hand on Veeck's shoulder, "he's just playing up to the crowd."

Who were playing up to him, cheering, egging him on.

Then pitcher Cain came to Veeck's rescue by really pitching to the midget, sending two fastballs speeding past Eddie before he could even think to swing.

"I wouldn't worry now," I said to Veeck.

Cain had started to laugh; he was almost collapsing with laughter, which the crowd aped, and he could barely throw at all as he tossed two more looping balls, three and then four feet over Eddie's head.

The littlest Brown trotted to his base as the crowd cheered and cameras clicked; then he stood with one foot on the bag as if he were thinking of stealing, which got a huge, roaring laugh.

Finally pinch runner Jim Delsing came over and Gaedel surrendered the base to him, giving the big man a comradely pat on the butt.

The crowd was going wild, Veeck grinning like a monkey, as I made my exit, to go down and meet my midget charge in Veeck's office. Eddie had his clothes changed—he was wearing a bright green and yellow shirt that made Veeck's taste seem mild—and I warned him that the reporters would be lying in wait.

"Veeck says it's your call," I said. "I can sneak you out of here—"

"Hell no!" Eddie was sitting on the floor, tying his shoes—he didn't need any help, this time. "It's great publicity! Man, I felt like Babe Ruth out there."

"Eddie, you're now what most every man in the country wishes he could be."

"Yeah? What's that?"

"A former major-leaguer."

Since Veeck had been talking about using Gaedel again, the little guy really warmed up to the reporters waiting outside the stadium, telling them "two guys I'd really like to face on the mound are Bob Feller and Dizzy Trout."

But it didn't work out that way. First off, despite the midget ploy, the Browns lost 6–2 to the Tigers, anyway. And before Veeck could put Gaedel into a White Sox game in Eddie's hometown of Chicago a month later, the baseball commissioner banned midgets from baseball.

Veeck had responded to Commissioner Harridge by saying, "Fine, but first you gotta establish what a midget is—is it three foot six, like Eddie? If it's five six, great! We can get rid of Phil Rizzuto!" The commissioner's ban was not only complete, but retroactive: Eddie didn't even make it into the record books, the Gaedel name nowhere to be seen in the official 1951 American League batting records—though the base-on-balls was in Cain's record, and a pinch-running appearance in Delsing's.

Nonetheless, this stuffed-shirt revisionist history did no good at all: record book or not, Eddie was immortal over Bill Veeck's stunt, and so was Bill Veeck.

Immortal in the figurative sense, of course. Their fame didn't stop Veeck from staring death in the face, nor, apparently, had it spared little Eddie Gaedel from murder.

3

The Keurtz Funeral Home was one of those storefront numbers, with a fancy faux-stone facade in the midst of pawnshops and bars. This was on the South Side, Ashland and 48th, the business district of a working-class neighborhood of two-flats and modest frame houses, a hard pitch away from Comiskey Park.

I left my car three blocks down, on a side street, mulling over what I'd learned from several phone calls to contacts in the Coroner's Office and the Homicide Bureau. The death had never been considered a possible homicide, so there'd been virtually no investigation.

A midget had died in his sleep, a not uncommon occurrence, considering the limited life expectancy of little people. Yes, there'd been some bruises, but Gaedel was known as a rough customer, a barroom brawler, with several assaults on his record. The unspoken but strongly implied thread was that if Gaedel hadn't died of natural causes, he'd earned whatever he'd gotten.

The alcove of the funeral home was filled with smoke and midgets. This was not surprising, the smoke anyway, being fairly typical for a Chicago storefront funeral parlor—no smoking was allowed in the visitation areas, so everybody crowded out in the entryway and smoked and talked.

Seeing all those small, strange faces turned toward me, as I entered, was unsettling: wrinkled doll faces, frowning at my six-foot presence, the men in suits and ties, the women in

Sunday best, like children playing dress up. I took off my hat, nodded at them as a group, and they resumed their conversations, a high-pitched chatter, like half a dozen Alvin and the Chipmunks records were playing simultaneously.

The dark-paneled visitation area was large, and largely empty, and just inside the door was the tiny coffin with Eddie peacefully inside. He wore a conservative suit and tie, hands folded; it was the only time I hadn't seen Eddie in a loud sport shirt, with the exception of that kid-size Browns uniform. Quite a few flowers were on display, many with Catholic trappings, a horseshoe arrangement ribboned MY FAVORITE BATTER—BILL VEECK prominent among them.

The folding chairs would have seated several hundred, but only two were occupied. Over to the right, a petite but normal-sized woman in black dabbed her eyes with a hanky as a trio of midgets—two men and a woman—stood consoling her. Eddie's mother, no doubt.

The female midget was maybe four feet and definitely quite lovely, a shapely blue-eyed blonde lacking pinched features or ungainly limbs, a miniature beauty in a blue satin prom dress. She was upset, weeping into her own hanky.

In the back sat a human non sequitur, a slim, rangy mourner in his late thirties, with rugged aging-American-boy good looks—anything but a midget. His expression somber, his sandy hair flecked with gray, he looked familiar to me, though I couldn't place him.

Since Eddie's mom was occupied, I wandered back to the full-size mourner and he stood, respectfully, as I approached.

"Nate Heller," I said, extending a hand. "I take it you were a friend of Eddie's, too. Sorry I can't place you...."

"Bob Cain," he said, shaking my hand.

"The pitcher!"

His smile was embarrassed. "That's right. You're a friend of Bill Veeck's, aren't you?"

"Yeah. I've done a number of jobs for Bill ... including body-guarding Eddie for that stunt, way back when."

Cain smiled again, a bittersweet expression. Then he moved over one and gestured to the empty chair, saying, "Sit down, won't you?"

We sat and talked. I was aware that Cain, after a contract squabble shortly following the midget incident, had been traded at Veeck's request to the Browns. Cain played the '52 and '53 seasons for him.

"Bill's a great guy," Cain said. "One owner who treated the players like human beings."

"Even if he did embarrass you?"

"That's just part of the Veeck package. Funny thing is, in the time I played for him, Bill never mentioned the midget thing. But I always wondered if he'd traded for me to make it up to me, or something. Anyway, I had a fine career, Mr. Heller."

"Nate."

"Beat the Yankees fifteen oh, in my first major league start. Pitched a one-hitter against Feller. I had a lot of good experiences in baseball."

"But you'll be remembered for pitching to a midget."

"At least I'll be remembered. It's part of baseball history, Nate—there'll never be another midget in the game ... just Eddie."

"Did you stay in touch with the little guy?"

"Naw.... I haven't seen him since I pitched against him. But when I read about this, I just had to pay my respects, as a good Christian, you know—to a man who was so important in my life."

"Are you still in the game, Bob?"

"Not since '56 ... got a calcium deposit on my wrist, and couldn't get my pitch back. I drove up from Cleveland for this—felt kind of ... obligated."

I didn't hear anything but sincerity in his words and his voice; but I would check up on Cain's whereabouts—and see if he'd driven up from Cleveland before or after Eddie's murder.

The petite blonde was standing at the casket, lingering there, staring down at Eddie, weeping softly into her hanky. The two men had gone back out to the alcove.

This left Mrs. Gaedel free, and I went over to her, introducing myself.

"Mrs. Gaedel, Bill Veeck sends his condolences," I told her, taking the seat next to her.

A pleasant-looking woman of sixty, salt-and-pepper hair in a bun, Mrs. Gaedel sat and listened as I told her how I'd been involved with Eddie in his famous stunt. I left out the part about the college girls in the lounge car.

"Mr. Veeck was wonderful to Eddie over the years," she said, her voice bravely strong. "Gave Eddie so much work. Eddie supported me, after his father died, you know."

"Eddie kept busy."

"Yes. TV, movies, stage.... He lived with me, you know—had his little apartment with its little furnishings in the attic ... ceiling so low I had trouble cleaning up there, but he loved it. That's where I found him ... in bed...."

I slipped an arm around her as she wept.

Then after a while I said, "You spoke to Mr. Veeck on the phone, I understand."

"Yes—this morning."

"I'm a private investigator, Mrs. Gaedel, and Bill asked me to talk to you about these ... doubts you have, about the circumstances of your son's death."

"Oh! Are you willing to look into that for me?"

"Bill has hired me to do that very thing, as long as we have your blessing."

"Of course you have my blessing! And my eternal thanks.... What do you want to know, Mr. Heller?"

"This is hardly the time, Mrs. Gaedel. I can come to your home, after the service sometime, in a day or two perhaps—"

"No, please, Mr. Heller. Let's talk now, if we could."

I was turning my hat in my hands like a wheel. "Actually, that would be wise, if you're up to it. The sooner I can get started—"

"I'm up to it. Start now."

We were interrupted several times, as Eddie's friends paid their respects. But her story was this: Eddie had been drinking heavily lately, and running with a rough crowd, who hung out at the Midgets' Club.

I knew this bar, which was over on Halstead, and dated back to the '40s; it had begun as a gimmick, a bar where the customers were served by midgets, mostly former members of the Singer Midgets who'd played Munchkins in *The Wizard of Oz*. An area was given over to small tables and short stools, for midget clientele, and eventually the midgets essentially took over. But for the occasional tourist who stopped by for the oddity of the joint—to pick up the trademark half-books of matches, see a few framed *Oz* photos, and get some Munchkin autographs—the Midgets' Club became the cultural center of midget activity in Chicago.

"I thought the Midgets' Club was pretty respectable," I said.

"It is—Elmer St. Aubin and his wife still run the place. But a rough element—carny types—hang out there, you know."

"That blonde you were talking to. She doesn't seem part of that element."

"She isn't, not all. That's Betsy Jane Perkins ... she worked with Eagle's Midget Troupe, does a lot of television, personal appearances, dressed and made up like a doll ... the 'Living Doll,' they call her."

"Were your son and Miss Perkins good friends?"

"Oh yes. He'd been dating her. She was wonderful. Best thing in his life ... I was so hopeful her good influence would wrest him away from that bad crowd."

"Do you suspect anyone in particular, Mrs. Gaedel?"

"No, I ... I really didn't know many of my son's friends. Betsy Jane is an exception. Another possibility are these juvenile delinquents."

"Oh?"

"That's what I think may have happened—a gang of those terrible boys may have gotten ahold of Eddie and beaten him."

"Did he say so?"

"No, not really. He didn't say anything, just stumbled off to bed."

"Had he been robbed, mugged? Was money missing from his wallet?"

She shook her head, frowning. "No. But these juveniles pick on the little people all the time. If my son were inebriated, he would have been the perfect target for those monsters. You should strongly consider that possibility."

"I will. Mrs. Gaedel, I'll be in touch with you later. My deepest sympathies, ma'am."

She took my hand and squeezed it. "God bless you, Mr. Heller."

In the alcove, I signed the memorial book. The crowd of midgets was thinning, and the blonde was gone.

Nothing left for me to do but follow the Yellow Brick Road.

4

The Midgets' Club might have been any Chicago saloon: a bar at the left, booths at the right, scattering of tables between, pool table in back, wall-hung celebrity photos here and there, neon beer signs burning through the fog of tobacco smoke, patrons chatting, laughing, over a jukebox's blare. But the bar was sawed-off with tiny stools, the tables and chairs and booths all scaled down to smaller proportions (with a few normal-sized ones up front, for tourist traffic), the pool table half-scale, the celebrity photos of Munchkins, the chatter and laughter of patrons giddy and high-pitched. As for the jukebox, Sinatra's "Tender Trap" was playing at the moment, to be followed by more selections running to slightly dated swing material, no rock or R & B—which suited me, and was a hell of a lot better than "Ding Dong the Witch Is Dead."

I had known the club's proprietor and chief bartender, Pernell "Little Elmer" St. Aubin, since he was, well, little—a child entertainer at the Midget Village at the Chicago World's Fair back in '33. He'd been tap dancing and I'd been busting pickpockets. Elmer had been in his teens when he appeared in *The Wizard of Oz*, so now—as he stood behind the bar, polishing a glass, a wizened Munchkin in an apron—he was probably only in his midthirties. But as was so often the case with his kind, he looked both older and younger than his years.

I selected one of the handful of somewhat taller stools at the bar and said to Elmer, "For a weekday, you're doing good business."

"It's kind of a wake," Elmer explained. "For Eddie Gaedel. People coming over after visitation at Keurtz's. You knew Eddie, didn't you?"

"Yeah. I was over there myself. Paying my respects, and Bill Veeck's."

Elmer frowned. "Couldn't Veeck make it himself?"

"He's pretty sick. So was Eddie ornery as ever, up to the end?"

"Christ yes! I hated serving that little bastard. Sweet enough guy sober, but what a lousy drunk. If I hadn't been secretly watering his drinks, over the years, he'd have busted up the joint long ago."

"I hear he may have been rolled by some juvies. Think that's what killed him?"

"I doubt it. Eddie carried a straight razor—people knew he did, too. I think these young punks woulda been scared to get cut. Funny thing, though."

"What is?"

"His mama said that straight razor didn't turn up in his things."

I thought about that, then asked, "So how *do* you think Eddie died?"

"I have my own opinion."

"Like to share that opinion, Elmer?"

"The cops weren't interested. Why are you?"

"Eddie was a friend. Maybe I'm just curious. Maybe there's a score to settle."

"Are you gonna drink something, Heller?"

I gave the Munchkin a ten, asked for a rum and Coke and told him he could keep the change, if he stayed chatty.

"Eddie was playing a puppet on a local kids' show," Elmer said, serving me up. "But he lost the gig 'cause of his boozing. So lately he was talking to some of my less classier clientele about going out on the carny circuit. Some kinda sideshow scam where they pretended to be Siamese triplets or something."

"Work is work."

"See that little dame over there?"

Every dame in here was little, but Elmer was talking about Betsy Jane, the Living Doll in her blue satin prom dress. I hadn't spotted her when I came in—she was sitting alone in a booth, staring down into a coffee cup cupped in her dainty hands.

Elmer leaned in conspiratorially. "That's Betsy Jane Perkins, the actress—Eddie was crazy about her, and she felt the same about him. She was trying to straighten him out, and I think she might've succeeded, if it hadn't been for that ex-husband of hers."

"Yeah?"

"Guy named Fred Peterson. He's a shrimp."

"A midget?"

"No, a *shrimp*—a 'normal'-size guy who stands just under five feet. He's a theatrical agent, still is Betsy Jane's agent; specializes in booking little people. Makes him feel like a big man, lording it over us."

"He is a regular?" I swiveled on the stool and glanced around. "Is he here?"

"Yes, he's a regular, no, he's not here. He wouldn't pay his respects to Eddie, that's for goddamn sure."

"Why?"

"Lately Fred's been trying to get back in Betsy Jane's good graces, among other things. Why don't you talk to her? She's a sweet kid. I think she'd do anything to help out where Eddie's concerned."

I took Elmer's advice, and my rum and Coke and I went over and stood next to the booth where the painfully pretty little woman gloomily sat. She looked up at me with beautiful if bloodshot blue eyes; her heavy, doll-like makeup was a little grief-smeared, but she was naturally pretty, with a fairly short, Marilyn-ish do.

"Miss Perkins, my name is Nate Heller—I was a friend of Eddie Gaedel's."

"I don't remember Eddie mentioning you, Mr. Heller," she said, almost primly, her voice a melodic soprano with a vibrato of sorrow.

"I'm an associate of Bill Veeck's. I escorted Eddie to that famous game in St. Louis back in '51."

She had brightened at the mention of Veeck's name, and was already gesturing for me to sit across from her.

"I saw you at the funeral parlor," she said, "talking to Helen."

"Helen?"

"Mrs. Gaedel."

"Yes. She feels the circumstances of her son's death are somewhat suspicious."

The blue eyes lowered. "I'd prefer to reminisce about Eddie and the fun times, the good times, than ..."

"Face the truth?"

"Mr. Heller, I don't know what happened to Eddie. I just know I've lost him, right when I thought ..." She began to cry, and got in her purse, rustling for a handkerchief.

I glanced over at Elmer, behind the bar, and he was squinting at me, making a vaguely frantic gesture that I didn't get. Shrugging at him, I returned my attention to the Living Doll.

"You'd been trying to help Eddie. Encourage him to stop drinking, I understand. Not run with such a rough crowd."

"That's right."

I'd hoped for elaboration.

I tried venturing down a different avenue. "I understand some JDs have been preying on little people in this neighborhood."

"That ... that's true."

"Eddie might have been beaten and robbed."

"Yes ... he might have."

"But you don't think that's the case, do you?"

Now she was getting a compact out of her purse, checking her makeup. "If you'll excuse me, Mr. Heller—I look a fright."

And she went off to the ladies' room.

I just sat there and sipped my rum and Coke, wondering if I would get anything out of Betsy Jane except tears, when an unMunchkinlike baritone growled at me.

"You got a fetish, pal?"

I turned and looked up at the source of the irritation, and the reason for Elmer's motioning to me: he was short, but no midget, possibly five foot, almost handsome, with a Steve Canyon jaw compromised by pugged nose and cow eyes; his hair was dark blond and slicked back and he wore a mustache that would have been stylish as hell if this were 1935. Deeply tanned, his build was brawny, his hairy, muscular chest shown off by the deep V-neck cut of his pale green herringbone golf shirt, his arms short but muscular.

I said, "What?"

"You got a scratch to itch, buddy?"

"What the hell are you talking about?"

He leaned in, eyes popping, teeth bared, cords in his neck taut; he reeked of Old Spice. "You some kind of pervert, pops? Some kinda letch for the midget ladies?"

Very quietly, I said, "Back off."

Something about how I'd said it gave him pause, and the clenched fist that was his face twitched a couple times, and he and his Old Spice aura backed away—but he kept standing there, muscular arms folded now, like a stubby, pissed-off genie.

"And you must be Fred Peterson," I said.

"Who wants to know?"

Not offering a hand to shake, I said, "My name's Heller— friend of Eddie Gaedel's, and Bill Veeck's."

He blinked. "What, you were over at the funeral home?"

"That's right."

"Paying your respects."

"Yes. And looking into Eddie's murder."

He frowned; then he scrambled across from me into the booth, where Betsy Jane had been sitting. "What do you mean, murder?"

"He was beaten to death, Fred. You don't mind if I call you 'Fred' ...?"

His hands were folded, but squeezing, as if he were doing isometrics. "The cops said it was natural causes. Why's it your business, the cops say it's natural causes?"

"I'm a private investigator, working for Veeck. When I get enough evidence, I'll turn it over to the cops and see if I can't change their minds about how 'natural' those causes were."

He leaned forward, hands still clasped, a vein in his forehead jumping. "Listen, that little prick had a big mouth and a lot of enemies. You're gonna get nowhere!"

I shrugged, sipped my rum and Coke. "Maybe I can get somewhere with Betsy Jane."

The cow eyes flashed. "Stay away from her."

"Why should I? She seems to like me, and I like her. She's a cute kid. She interests me ... kind of a new frontier."

"I said stay away."

"Who died and appointed you head of the Lollipop Guild? I'm going to find out who killed Eddie Gaedel, and have myself some tight little fun along the way."

And I grinned at him, until he growled a few obscenities and bolted away, heading toward the rear of the bar, almost bumping into Betsy Jane, coming back from the restroom. She froze seeing him, and he clutched her by the shoulders and got right in her face and said something to her, apparently something unpleasant, even threatening. Then he stalked toward the rear exit.

Her expression alarmed, she took her seat across from me and said, "You should go now."

"That was your agent, right?"

" ... right."

"And your boyfriend?"

"No ... husband. Ex-husband. Please go."

"Jealous of you and Eddie, by any chance? Did you go to him with the idea for a new act, you and Eddie as boy and girl livin' dolls?"

She shook her head, blonde bangs shimmering. "Mr. Heller, you don't know what kind of position you're putting me in...."

I knew that her ex-husband didn't want any man putting this doll in any position.

But I said, "I think for a little guy, your ex-husband and current agent has a tall temper. And I think he's goddamn lucky the cops didn't investigate this case, because he makes one hell of a suspect in Eddie's death."

She began to weep again, but this was different, this was more than grief—there was fear in it.

"What do you know, Betsy Jane?"

"Nuh ... nothing ... nothing...."

"Tell me. Just tell me—so that *I* know. I won't take anything to the police without your permission."

Damp eyelashes fluttered. "Well ... I ... I don't know anything, except that ... on that last night, Fred was ... nice to Eddie and me."

"Nice?"

"Yes. He'd been furious with me, at the suggestion that Eddie and I would work as a team, livid that I would suggest that he, of all people, should book such an act.... We had two, no three, terrible arguments about it. Then ... then he changed. He can do that, run hot and cold. He apologized, said he'd been a jerk, said he wanted to make it up, wanted to help. Sat and talked with us all evening, making plans about the act."

"Go on."

"That's all."

"No it isn't. I can see it in those pretty eyes, Betsy Jane. The rest ... tell me the rest."

She swallowed, nodded, sighed. "They ... they left together. Eddie lived close, you know, easy walk home to his mother's house—Fred was going to talk business with him. They went out the back way, around midnight. It was the last time I saw Eddie alive."

The alley behind the bar, bumped up against the backyards of residences, would be as good a place as any for an assault.

She was saying, "But I can't imagine Fred would do such a thing."

"Sure you can."

She shook her head. "Anyway, Eddie was no pushover. He carried a straight razor, you know."

"So I hear. But I also hear it wasn't among his effects."

"Oh, Eddie had it that night. I saw it."

"Yeah?"

"He emptied his pocket, looking for change for the jukebox ... laid his things right on this counter, razor among them. We were sitting in this very booth ... this was ... *our* booth."

She began to cry again, and I got over on her side of the booth, slid an arm around her, and comforted her, thinking that she really was a cute kid, and midget sex was definitely on my short list of things yet undone in a long and varied life.

But more to the point, what had become of that razor? If Fred had attacked Eddie out back, maybe that razor had been dropped in the scuffle—and if it was back there, somewhere, I'd have the evidence I needed to get the cops to open an investigation.

"Betsy Jane," I said, "we'll talk again ... when you're feeling up to it."

"All right ... but Mr. Heller ... Nate ... I am afraid. Terribly afraid."

I squeezed her shoulder, kissed her cheek. "I'll make the bad man go away."

She put her hand on my thigh—her little bitty hand. Christ, it felt weird. Also, good.

Nodding to Elmer, I headed toward the rear exit, and stepped out into the alley. The night was moonless with a scattering of stars, and the lighting was negligible—no streetlamps back here, just whatever scant illumination spilled from the frame houses whose backyards bordered the asphalt strip. A trio of garbage cans—full-scale, nothing midget about them—stood against the back of the brick building, and some empty liquor and beer cartons were stacked nearby.

Not much to see, and in the near-darkness, I would probably need my flashlight to probe for that missing straight razor. I had just decided to walk the several blocks to the side street where my car was parked, to get the flash, when a figure stepped out from the recess of an adjacent building's rear doorway.

"Looking for something?" Fred Peterson asked, those cow eyes wide and wild, teeth bared like an angry animal, veins throbbing in his neck, one hand behind his back. Though he stood only five foot, his brawny frame, musculature obvious in the skintight golf shirt, made him a threatening presence as he stepped into the alley like a gunfighter out onto the Main Street of Dodge.

I was thinking how I should have brought my gun along—only usually, attending midget funerals, it wasn't necessary.

"Get some ideas," he said, "talking to Betsy Jane?"

He was standing there, rocking on legs whose powerful thighs stood out, despite the bagginess of his chinos.

Shrugging, I said, "I thought Eddie mighta dropped something when you jumped him."

Peterson howled as he whipped something from behind him and charged, it was a bat, he was wielding a goddamn baseball bat, and he was whipping it at me, slicing the air, the bat whooshing over me as I ducked under the swing. Screw baseball, I tackled him, taking him down hard, and the bat fell from his grasp, clattering onto the asphalt. I rolled off him, rolling toward the sound, and then I had the bat in my hands, as I got up and took my stance.

That's when I found that straight razor I'd been looking for, or rather Fred Peterson showed me what had become of it, as he yanked it from his pocket and swung it around, the meager light of the alley managing to wink off the shining blade.

I didn't wait for him to come at me: I took my swing.

The bat caught him in the side of the head, a hard blow that caved his skull in, and by the time Peterson fell to his knees, his motor responses were dead, and so was he. He flopped forward, on his face, razor spilling from limp fingers, blood and brains leaching out onto the asphalt as I stood over him, the bat resting against my shoulder.

"Strike zone my ass," I said to nobody, breathing hard.

Finally I went back into the Midgets' Club, carrying the bloody bat, getting my share of my looks, though Betsy Jane had gone. I leaned on the bar and told Elmer to call the cops.

But the little bartender just looked at me in amazement. "What the hell did you do, Heller?"

"Somebody had to go to bat for Eddie. Call the goddamn cops, would you, please?"

5

No charges were brought against me—my actions were clearly in self-defense—and Eddie Gaedel's death is listed to this day as "natural causes" on the books. Though I shared with them everything I knew about the matter, the police simply didn't want to go to the trouble of declaring Eddie a murder victim, merely to pursue a deceased suspect. Poor Eddie just couldn't get a fair shake in any of the record books.

A few days after the cops cleared me, Veeck spoke to me on the phone, from a room in the Mayo Clinic.

"You know, ten years ago, when I sent Eddie Gaedel into that game," he said, reflectively, "I knew it would be that little clown's shining moment ... what I didn't know was that it would be mine, too! Hell, I knew it was a good gag, that the fans would roar, and the stuffed shirts holler. But who coulda guessed it'd become the single act forever identified with me?"

"We're any of us lucky to be remembered for anything, Bill," I said.

"Yeah. Yeah. Suppose Eddie felt that way?"

"I know he did."

For years after, Helen Gaedel remembered me at Christmas with cookies or a fruitcake. Betsy Jane Perkins was grateful, too.

Veeck expressed his gratitude by paying me handsomely, and, typically, fooled himself and all of us by not dying just yet. The man who invented fan appreciation night, who provided a day-care center for female employees before the term was coined, who was first to put the names of players on the backs of uniforms, who broke the color line in the American League, and who sent a midget up to bat—and who also bought back the Chicago White Sox in 1975—lived another irascible fifteen years.

And wasn't that a hell of a stunt.

I OWE THEM ONE

My friend and research associate George Hagenauer provided his usual stellar support on these short novels. In particular, on "Dying in the Post-War World," he put in hours of newspaper research, took me on a walking tour of the various crime scenes, and developed the background for the character Otto Bergstrum.

"Dying in the Post-War World" is based on a real case, but (with the exception of Bill Drury and a few minor police officials), the characters are wholly fictional and are not intended to be representations of their real-life counterparts. The time frame of the novel differs somewhat from that of the real crimes, and the aspect involving the very real Sam Giancana is fanciful. My solution to this famous case is also fanciful, although (like Nate Heller) I have come to the conclusion that it is unlikely that William Heirens—the real-life convicted Lipstick Killer—was truly guilty of the kidnapping and murder of young Susan Degnan. George Hagenauer doubts that Heirens is guilty of any of the murders.

The short novel "Kisses of Death" has an extensive basis in history, but liberties have been taken with facts, including compression of time. Most of the characters are real people and appear under their true names. George suggested this subject matter and helped gather research material.

In addition to contemporary newspaper accounts of the Bodenheim murders, and "A Malady of the Soul," a 1981 *Chicago Reader* article by Michael Miner, the following books were of help: *Ben Hecht: The Man Behind the Legend* (1990) by William MacAdams; *Chicago Renaissance* (1966) by Dale Kramer; *A Child of the Century* (1954) by Ben Hecht; *The Five Lives of Ben Hecht* (1977) by Don Fetherling; *My Life and Loves in Greenwich Village* (1954) by Maxwell Bodenheim; and *A Treasury of Ben Hecht* (1959), which includes his play "Winkelberg," based on Bodenheim's life.

Thanks also to my wife, writer Barbara Collins, a Marilyn Monroe expert, for contributing her insights. Of dozens of Monroe volumes consulted, the most useful was *The Unabridged Marilyn—Her Life from A to Z* (1987). Readers are encouraged to seek out our collaborative novel, *Bombshell* (2004), also about Marilyn Monroe, and the Heller novel *Bye Bye, Baby* (2011), about the murder of the actress.

On "Strike Zone," George Hagenauer gets the MVP—he knew Bill Veeck and kept me honest in my depiction. Newspapers of the day were consulted, and a number of books, including *Bill Veeck: A Baseball Legend* (1988) by Gerald Eskenazi; *Munchkins of Oz* (1996) by Stephen Cox; *The Story of My Life* (1989) by Hank Greenberg; and *Veeck—As in Wreck* (1962; revised 1976) by Bill Veeck with Ed Linn.

My thanks to the original editors of these short novels, Louis Wilder, Doug Greene, and Otto Penzler.

Original publication:

"Dying in the Post-War World," *Dying in the Post-War World: A Nathan Heller Casebook* (1991), Foul Play Press.

"Kisses of Death," *Kisses of Death: A Nathan Heller Casebook* (2001), Crippen & Landru.

"Strike Zone," *Murderer's Row* (2001), New Millennium Press.

ABOUT THE AUTHOR

Photo Credit: Bamford Studio

Max Allan Collins was hailed in 2004 by *Publisher's Weekly* as "a new breed of writer." A frequent Mystery Writers of America "Edgar" nominee in both fiction and nonfiction categories, he has earned an unprecedented sixteen Private Eye Writers of America "Shamus" nominations, winning for his Nathan Heller novels, *True Detective* (1983) and *Stolen Away* (1991), receiving the PWA life achievement award, the Eye, in 2007.

His graphic novel *Road to Perdition* (1998) is the basis of the Academy Award–winning 2002 film starring Tom Hanks, Paul Newman, and Daniel Craig, directed by Sam Mendes. It was followed by two acclaimed prose sequels, *Road to Purgatory* (2004) and *Road to Paradise* (2005), with a graphic novel sequel, *Return to Perdition*, forthcoming. He has written a number of innovative suspense series, notably Quarry (the first series about a hired killer) and Eliot Ness (four novels about the famous real-life Untouchable's Cleveland years). He is completing a number of Mike Hammer novels begun by the late Mickey Spillane, with whom Collins did many projects; the fourth of these, *Lady, Go*

Die!, is a 2012 publication. *No One Will Hear You*, a serial-killer thriller written with Matthew Clemens, was published in 2011.

His many comics credits include the syndicated strip "Dick Tracy"; his own "Ms. Tree" (longest-running private eye comic book); "Batman"; and *CSI: Crime Scene Investigation*, based on the hit TV series for which he has also written video games, jigsaw puzzles, and ten novels that have sold millions of copies worldwide.

Termed "the novelization king" by *Entertainment Weekly*, his tie-in books have appeared on the *USA Today* bestseller list nine times and the *New York Times* list three. His movie novels include *Saving Private Ryan, Air Force One,* and *American Gangster,* the latter winning the Best Novel "Scribe" Award in 2008 from the International Association of Tie-in Writers.

An independent filmmaker in the midwest, Collins has written and directed five features and two documentaries, including the Lifetime movie *Mommy* (1996) and a 1997 sequel, *Mommy's Day*. He wrote *The Expert*, a 1995 HBO World Premiere, and *The Last Lullaby*, starring Tom Sizemore, a feature film based on Collins' acclaimed novel, *The Last Quarry*; the latter film won numerous awards on the film festival circuit before its theatrical and home-video release.

His one-man show, "Eliot Ness: An Untouchable Life," was nominated for an Edgar for Best Play of 2004 by the Mystery Writers of America; a film version, written and directed by Collins, was released on DVD in 2008 and appeared on PBS stations in 2009. His documentary, *Caveman: V.T. Hamlin & Alley Oop*, was also released on DVD after screening on PBS stations.

His other credits include film criticism, short fiction, songwriting, trading-card sets, and a regular column in *Asian Cult Cinema* magazine. His nonfiction work has received many honors, with his coffee-table book *The History of Mystery* receiving nominations for every major mystery award and his recent *Men's Adventure Magazines* (with George Hagenauer) winning the Anthony Award.

Collins lives in Muscatine, Iowa, with his wife, writer Barbara Collins; they have collaborated on six novels and numerous short stories, and are currently writing the successful "Trash 'n' Treasures" mysteries—their *Antiques Flee Market* (2008) won the *Romantic Times* Best Humorous Mystery Novel award in 2009. Their son Nathan is a Japanese-to-English translator, working on video games, manga, and novels.